Blood Cursed
And Other Tales of
the Fantastic

By: Jamie Marchant

Jamie Marchant

ACKNOWLEDGEMENTS

The author wishes to express her extreme gratitude to the members of the Robrek Steele Conspiracy Writers' Group: Peg Daniels and Jim Elston. (I wrote the names in alphabetical order, so don't go quibbling about order of importance.) Peg and Jim supported me throughout all my writing. They said they deserved a full paragraph acknowledgement each (and they're right), but they'll have to settle for sharing the same paragraph and sharing that paragraph with Panera Bread who allows us to occupy a booth every Friday.

I wish to thank my husband Tim and son Jesse for their love and patience.

CONTENTS

PREFACE

The following is a collection of previously published short stories. I have gathered them into a single collection for the benefit of anyone who'd like to find them all in one place. If you enjoy the stories in this collection, please leave a review, and I am also happy to hear from my readers at jamie-marchant@jamie-marchant.com

BLOOD CURSED

Author Note: "Blood Cursed" was originally published in
Bards & Sages, April 2012.

No music greeted Pandaros as he entered Ares's temple
nor did the scent of incense as they would have in a temple to
Sulis, the goddess of his people. He seemed alone in the main
sanctuary, but he knew the acolytes of Ares watched through
hidden panels. Rumors claimed they waited for someone with
signs of weakness to enter. Then they'd pour forth, seize the
unfortunate, and sacrifice him to their god. Pandaros had
found no truth behind these rumors, but he knew that plenty
of animals and some criminals died on Ares's altar, bleeding
out their lives into the bowl at the foot of Ares's statue. It was
a hard death, both the blood and the pain feeding the magic of
Ares's priests.

Pandaros knelt at Ares's feet; the stench of blood from a
fresh sacrifice was nearly intolerable. The power in this place
was undeniable—dark and forbidding, nothing like the peace
and serenity found in Sulis's temples. It'd been five years
since he'd last been in a temple dedicated to Ares, five years
since he'd taken the vow never to kill again. But he'd broken
that vow for his daughter's sake. Making the vow had been as

wrong as breaking it. The first had nearly cost his daughter her life and her throne. The second had cost him his soul.

Pandaros drew one of the many knives secreted on his body, held his left arm over the sacrificial bowl, and sliced a new cut alongside the numerous scars that marked his forearm. As he bled, he felt the magic of the temple coalesce. His blood sizzled as it hit the bowl, and the wound on his arm healed instantly, signaling Ares's acceptance. Pandaros didn't know whether to be relieved or sickened.

A door opened behind Pandaros. He stood and faced the high priest of Ares. Zotico looked no older than he had the last time Pandaros had seen him; the priests of Ares never seemed to age. Zotico spread his arms wide in welcome. "Pandaros! How wonderful! Rumors said you were dead. Come in, come in." He gestured toward the doorway. "You've been a stranger far too long."

Zotico's enthusiasm seemed excessive even for him. Warily, Pandaros followed Zotico down the corridor to the high priest's office. Zotico gestured Pandaros into a chair and offered him a glass of Oenomel, a sweet mixture of honey and wine he'd never had the taste for. Zotico poured himself a glass and sat on the other side of the desk. "Pandaros, my friend, why have you neglected your obligations to Ares?"

"I have no obligation to your god."

Zotico shook his head in mock sadness. "Still you try to deny it? You've always worshipped Ares with your heart and your actions, even if you don't acknowledge him with your words."

Pandaros struggled to keep his face expressionless. The high priest was right: his hands were so stained with blood they'd never be clean. He'd tried to cleanse them when he made his vow, but he'd failed.

Zotico smiled. "Tell me, my son, where have you been?"

"Away."

Zotico laughed. "Long have I wished for the power of Delphi to penetrate your secrets. Is there a person in the world who knows even half of them?" Zotico paused; Pandaros said nothing. "I see my curiosity shall have to be contained. Ares is a harsh master and not given to satisfying mere curiosity. Still, he has rewarded my devotions: your presence here cannot be a coincidence. I'm in need of a mercenary for a special job."

"I'm not looking for work. I'll not kill again." Pandaros took a sip of the Oenomel; it tasted better than he remembered. Realizing how thirsty he was, he took a bigger gulp.

"Then why are you here?"

"To pay penance for my sins. I want to be sacrificed."

Zotico laughed. "Really, Pandaros, that would be a waste of talent. Your life is a better service to Ares than your death would be."

Pandaros tightened his fists. "I'm not doing this for Ares's sake, but my own. It is the only fit way for a life like mine to end."

Zotico laughed again, and Pandaros wanted to grab the priest's tongue and tear it out. "A life that has brought pain and suffering ending in pain and suffering. It does seem appropriate, and I'd be happy to oblige you, but I know of no other who can accomplish the job I have at hand."

"That's not my problem."

Zotico spread his hands wide. "Indulge me for a moment. If after I've finished you still feel the same way, I will oblige you."

Pandaros merely grunted. The most tiresome part of dealing with Zotico was the high priest's love of the sound of his own voice.

"First, are you up on the current political situation?"

"Not really. I care little about the Saloynan king."

"King Frare's still hanging onto power by his fingernails and getting increasingly paranoid. He had his oldest executed not six months ago. Treason, he claimed. It could be true, but not likely. What is true is that Crown Prince Nicanor had the misfortune to reach the age at which Frare did away with his old man. Prince Rasmus is now the crown prince and heir. Do you know the young prince?"

Pandaros shrugged. When he'd left the country five years ago, Prince Rasmus had been a child of fourteen.

Feeling unexpectedly sleepy, Pandaros yawned. He glanced at the high priest's goblet, untouched. Cursing his carelessness, he tried to rise, but he fell to the floor as the darkness overtook him.

* * *

When Pandaros awoke, he found himself chained to the wall in a small cell, lit only by torches flickering in the hallway. He felt pain in his biceps and calves. He looked down to see small, fresh cuts. Blood fueled all the magic of Ares's priests, and Zotico had taken his. Worse, all of his weapons had been found and taken. Then he felt the edges of panic, as he realized he could no longer feel the wax on his face; he'd carefully concealed the scars he'd received as a prisoner of the Massossinans.

Shortly, Zotico arrived, accompanied by a couple well-armed acolytes. "Pandaros, or should I call you Darhour? Imagine my surprise when I had the wax and cosmetics cleaned off your face and found that two of my favorite mercenaries are actually the same man. How many of my other favorites are you?"

"What have you done to me?" Pandaros looked at the cuts on his arms and legs.

"I apologize if you find my behavior impolite. Your arrival was so fortuitous I truly had no choice. A most influential client requires a service, and I can think of no other with the necessary skills. So I've used your blood to place a curse on you. Do as ordered, or you will die."

Pandaros sneered, "I've already told you I want to die. Find another killer."

"I was afraid that would be your attitude. But once you die, the curse will spread to those who share your blood. Have you family, Pandaros?"

Rage twisted Pandaros's features, and he strained at the chains, eager to get his hands around Zotico's throat. He'd allow no harm come to Samantha, the daughter he'd sired with the Korthlundian queen.

The priest's smile broadened. "I see you do. You'll meet the client in the morning. Try to have a good rest." He left the cell, followed by the acolytes.

Pandaros tried to relax into a meditative state, but his rage was so great that it took nearly an hour. Then, slowly and painfully, he dislocated his thumbs. He slipped free of the manacles and popped his joints back in place. Then he combed through his long hair, removing a metal barb Zotico had missed while disarming him. He picked the lock and exited the cell. The torches in the corridor had been put out, but that was no impediment to him. In his former life as an assassin for the father of the present king, he'd had magic performed on his eyes, giving him the ability to see in the dark. He crept through the basement corridors of the temple, quietly opening doors until he found the room where they'd stored his weapons. He re-secreted his six knives in various places on his body and buckled on his sword, feeling more at ease now that he was armed again.

He wanted to creep through the temple until he found the high priest's rooms. He palmed a knife, eager to use it to slit the high priest's throat. I'll not be his puppet, allowing him to pull my strings. But his only choice was to wait. If the high priest placed the blood curse on him, only he could remove it. Pandaros had sworn never to kill again, but no one would touch his daughter. He'd made sure the duke who threatened her throne learned that lesson well. He remembered how good it felt to kill him.

Pandaros threw a knife, and Duke Argblutal's underling fell face-down into the room. Pandaros stepped over the body.

"Guards!" the duke yelled.

Pandaros laughed. "There are no guards to hear you. I've been most thorough."

The duke grabbed his sword. "Do you honestly think you're my match?" he sneered.

"Easily." Pandaros drew his sword. He could have killed the duke with a throwing knife, but that would have been too quick, too easy. The monster had to be made to feel all the pain he'd caused Samantha. That wasn't possible, though. It took a heart to suffer as she had. Pandaros lunged in for a quick attack. The duke parried, but Pandaros's sword made a shallow slice across the duke's upper arm.

"You think the people will bow before a bastard?" the duke taunted, but Pandaros didn't answer. Words were wasted breath. Relentlessly, he battered the duke back toward the wall. Blood sprang from wounds on the duke's legs and arms. Pandaros was vaguely aware the duke had scored a few hits of his own, but in the heat of battle he never felt pain.

The duke was weakening, and he again yelled for assistance. His parries became wilder and clumsier, and Pandaros saw his opening. He swung his sword toward the duke's stomach, slicing open his midsection and spilling his entrails. The duke clutched at his guts and dropped to his knees. Pandaros bent down beside him.

The duke gasped. "Do you really think you can put your bastard on the throne? Do you think they will bend the knee to the daughter of a stable groom?"

"You'll never know if they do or not." Pandaros prodded the duke's intestines with his sword. "You could take three days to die of such wounds. It's a pity I can't spare the time to watch." He drew a knife. "I've heard you remove the manhood of those who disappoint you."

He'd been right to kill the duke. Samantha was the one good thing he'd done with his life, and because of him, she'd reign as queen of Korthlundia. So why did he feel such guilt in the breaking of his vow? He knew the answer. Not only would the goddess be displeased, but his daughter would be ashamed of him; she'd taught him to value life. He could no longer kill without conscience, not even a monster like Argblutal.

* * *

In the morning, Zotico laughed when he found the empty cell. "I should have known the manacles couldn't hold you. Where are you hiding?"

Pandaros stepped out of a nearby room and put his sword at Zotico's back. "How did you know I was still here?"

Zotico turned around slowly but looked more amused than frightened. "I know men, Pandaros. You have someone, a child, I believe, you would not allow to be harmed. Put that sword away and come with me to my office. Your client awaits."

Resenting the necessity, Pandaros sheathed his sword. When they arrived at the high priest's office, Zotico preceded him inside. Pandaros stopped in the doorway as he recognized his client. Prince Rasmus had always been fond of horses and had spent a good deal of time in the stables. Hiding his true place in the king's household as an assassin, Pandaros had played the role of assistant master of the horse.

"You?" the prince said. Rasmus turned to Zotico. "I need the best available, and you bring me my father's stable groom."

"No, I bring you your grandfather's chief assassin."

Both Pandaros's and the prince's eyes widened. "Nobody knows The Ghost's identity!" the prince protested. "How can you know he's telling the truth?"

Pandaros had also thought his identity as The Ghost a secret, one he'd intended to take to his grave. Would he now have to kill both Zotico and the prince? Or did his identity even matter anymore? After all, he planned to die when this was finished.

"I never said I was The Ghost," Pandaros objected.

Zotico smiled. "Will you swear on your child's blood that you are not?"

Pandaros glared at Zotico; one didn't swear false by blood to a priest of Ares. The harm that could come from such a false oath was incalculable.

"I assure you, Your Highness, Pandaros was your grandfather's assassin, and he can still walk through walls. Last night I left him chained in the basement cell, and this morning I found him out of his cell waiting to stab me in the back. He is the best man to accomplish your job, the only man."

The prince looked Pandaros over warily. "I should have known you didn't get those scars from tending horses." The prince referred to the horizontal lines carved in Pandaros's face. "I need you to kill my father."

"No!" Quick as thought, Pandaros grabbed the prince by the hair and put a knife to his throat. "You will remove the blood curse, Zotico, or His Highness dies."

"Now, now, it isn't that simple. To end the curse, I require blood shed by your hand."

"I'll slit His Highness's throat, and you can use his blood."

Zotico smiled as if he were indulging a small child. "You say you will not kill, yet now you threaten an innocent. Put that knife away before you do something all three of us will regret."

Pandaros knew he wouldn't kill the young prince, but he kept the knife steady. "Why should I kill the king?"

Zotico shook his head. "Do you have to ask?"

"Please," the prince said. "My father had my brother murdered simply out of paranoia. How long before he decides it's my turn?"

Pandaros paused. Frare had been clearly insane five years ago. How much worse had he grown since? "Will you be a better king than your father?"

"How could I be worse? The people starve while he pursues his endless wars with Massossina."

"You would change this?"

"I would do everything in my power to."

Pandaros sized up the prince. Would he be the type of ruler Samantha would be? Pandaros thought not, but even at fourteen, the young prince had had a concern for the people, which his father didn't share.

Zotico stepped toward Pandaros. "Is an insane king worth the life of your child?"

Pandaros glared at the high priest. If he had to kill someone for Samantha to be safe, he'd do it. Why not let it be someone who deserved to die? He removed the knife from the prince's throat and relaxed his hold. The prince pulled away, rubbing his throat. He showed surprising dignity for one so young. But why should he be surprised? Samantha, too, was just nineteen.

"Tell me your father's habits, as thoroughly as possible."

Zotico gestured to the chairs. "Please, let us do this over breakfast."

When they were seated around the high priest's desk and acolytes had delivered wine, fruit, and pastries, Prince Rasmus detailed his father's routine. "He has everything tasted before he eats or drinks. He has guards with him constantly, except at night when he sleeps with two large boarhounds. They'd tear a man to shreds at the slightest provocation." The prince gulped the wine, but Pandaros touched nothing. He'd not be careless a second time.

Pandaros continued to ask questions until a plan formed in his mind. "I'll need the livery of a palace servant," he said.

* * *

His face disguised again with wax and makeup and his hair dyed the same dark brown as the king's chief servant, Pandaros walked the streets from the temple to the palace. Five years had dulled his memory of the horrors of the Saloynan capital. Beggars were everywhere—young children and old men and women, emaciated and covered in running sores. There were no older children. Pandaros knew why. King Frare's troops swept regularly through the city, and all boys old enough were drafted into the army, all girls taken to brothels. Pandaros himself had been caught up in such a sweep when he was a nineteen-year-old foreigner; it had been the first step toward making him the killer he was.

As he walked, he contemplated the kill he was about to make. Physically, he didn't expect any difficulty. But the goddess hadn't given him the right to decide who lives and who dies. Samantha had taught him that. Still, for her sake, there was no turning back. He was already damned, but she would live free of his taint—a defect that had led him to find pleasure in the shedding of blood.

At dusk, Pandaros got to the opening to the drainage ditches that ran in a labyrinth under the palace. He slipped inside, the livery Prince Rasmus had provided secured in an oilcloth high on his back. Anyone else would be hopelessly lost in the ditches, but during the years he'd spent as the king's personal assassin, Pandaros had fully explored them and marked major passageways with symbols that had meaning only to him. His ability to see in the dark made a torch unnecessary. Most of the ditches were high enough that he could walk in a crouched position, but in places he had to crawl through the filth. The stench was enough to bring tears to his eyes.

After half an hour of slogging through the muck, he made it through to the grate that lay under the unused portion of the servants' quarters. Praying no one had noticed and tightened the grate since he'd last left it loose, Pandaros pushed upward. The rust of years had partially sealed the grate, but with a hard shove, he was able to loosen it. As silently as possible, he pushed it aside and climbed up into the corridor above. He replaced the grate and changed into the livery of a palace servant.

As The Ghost, Pandaros had learned that few paid attention to servants. As long as he walked openly and purposefully, he was close to invisible. In the palace laundry, Pandaros picked up a pile of linens. Carrying them through the servants' corridors helped to hide his face and made him look occupied. The Ghost hadn't been able to walk through walls as credited. Often, he'd walked into his victims' rooms in plain sight. He'd been seen, but not noticed.

* * *

Pandaros neared the quarters of the king's personal servants and got out his blowpipe. He opened the door and stepped inside. Three men sat playing cards. "Who are—?" one of them began, but before he could finish the question, Pandaros had dropped the linens, brought the blowpipe to his lips, and shot three darts—coated in a powerful sleeping potion—in quick succession, striking two of the three men. His skills rusty, he missed the third man, but he palmed and threw a knife as the man jumped up from the table. The servant toppled, the knife through his left eye. Pandaros felt sickened. Even as The Ghost, he'd always tried to kill no one but the target. Pandaros tied and gagged the living servants, then secured them in a closet.

He bent to retrieve his knife, getting his first good look at the servant he'd killed. He was little older than a boy, an innocent who hadn't deserved death. He knew Samantha would be appalled if she knew he'd cut short another life. Yet, recollecting the perfect throw of the knife caused a familiar rush to flood through him. Repulsed by his own emotions, he wiped his knife on the servant's shirt and hauled him into the closet.

On a tray on a nearby table, Pandaros spotted the decanter of brandy and a single glass. He had merely to wait for the king to ring for it to be delivered. He'd timed things so he shouldn't have long to wait. King Frare was a creature of habit.

When the bell rang, Pandaros picked up the tray. Anticipation rushed through him, the thrill of the hunt, which he knew would be followed by the sweet joy of the kill. Vilifying himself as a rabid dog in need of being put down, Pandaros left the servants' quarters.

When he reached the king's rooms, the guards barely looked at him, simply stood aside and allowed him to enter. King Frare sat at a desk with his back to the door, the boarhounds at his feet.

"Set it down over there." The king gestured without turning. The boarhounds, however, got to their feet and began a low growl. Before the growling could rise to anything more threatening, Pandaros hit each one with a dart from the blowpipe. The king turned, and Pandaros threw a knife, hitting King Frare square in the throat. The king gurgled and fell on top of his hounds.

Savoring the experience he'd gone too long without, Pandaros took out a vial and filled it with the king's blood. He'd almost forgotten how good the successful annihilation of a target felt. Once, he'd killed his daughter's enemy to keep her safe. Now, he'd taken another life for the same reason. He'd thought he'd be racked by guilt for again violating his vow, but he felt no such emotion. As he thought of the beggars' faces and fate of the Saloynan youth, he couldn't regret what he'd done. Who else could have managed the kill? Prince Rasmus would be a better ruler than his father. The death of the King Frare would lead to a better life for thousands, tens of thousands. Would not such a death be as pleasing to Sulis as it was to him? Weren't the deaths of certain men more valuable than their lives? Did he have the right to destroy his skill if it could be used for good?

Perhaps he wouldn't have himself sacrificed, after all.

AS LUCK WOULD HAVE IT

Author Note: "As Luck Would Have It" was originally published in *The World of Myth,* March 2012.

The trouble started this morning when I was making my way to back to my hovel. I was nearing my neighborhood when I heard the unmistakable m-m-m-r-r-o-o-w of a cat fight. Out of an alley shot a grey tabby chased by a large tom as dark as midnight. I'm not normally a superstitious person, and a black cat crossing my path wouldn't normally bother me, but in pursuing his rival this black cat twined himself around my legs, causing me to trip and slam my head into a three-foot high brick wall. Since I was already so close to the ground and the world was spinning, I deemed it appropriate to continue the rest of the way and lay still for a moment. At the time, I didn't realize the fall had torn my shirt, revealing a gold chain I had recently acquired.

"Are you alright, sir?" called a street urchin who'd been sleeping in the alley.

I groaned in response, certain I'd fractured my skull. Before I realized what was happening, little hands tugged at the chain, the clasp broke, and little feet took off running. I stumbled to my feet to see the child disappear around the corner. I'd scaled a five-story building and snuck through a window into a lady's chamber to acquire that chain, risking arrest and hanging, and I wasn't going to let some street child steal it from me. Besides, I couldn't countenance theft in one so young.

I had two problems in my plan to apprehend the villain. One was the cut above my eyebrow, causing blood to flow into my right eye, and the second was the still-spinning world. You must take this into account and not blame me too heavily for what happened next. Gamely, I took off in pursuit of the thieving scoundrel and rounded the corner. I did not see the ladder until it was too late to stop. Now, as I've said, I'm not normally a superstitious person, and I have run under many a ladder with impunity, but this time, because of the blood in my eye and my none-too-steady balance, I rammed my shoulder against one of the rungs, causing the ladder to topple and the workman using it to fall. I did my best to cushion his fall, seeing that he landed on top of me. Not only did this knock the air completely out of my lungs, but as I fell, my purse caught on the ladder and tore, scattering rings and other baubles.

The noise—the workman howling at the top of his lungs, as I might have been if I could catch a breath—drew a small crowd. "Well, well, well, what have we here," a voice said, as the workman was helped off of me. "If it isn't young Phineus."

To my horror, I discovered the voice belonged to Constable Rawlins. The good constable had been trying to apprehend me for some time, but when the world was not spinning and I could see out of both eyes, I was—and I can say this without boasting—the fastest runner in the city of Longston Beachidea. A hand grabbed me and hauled me roughly to my feet while I was still struggling to get air back into my lungs.

Believing my neck sufficiently long without having it stretched, I desperately scanned my surroundings for a way to extricate myself from my predicament. That was when I saw it. An owl flying in the daylight is the worst kind of luck and a sure death omen, but since I'm not a superstitious man, I didn't fear for myself. Instead, I pointed. "Hey, look, it's an owl."

The owl conveniently hooted to confirm its identity. Fortunately, the crowd, especially Constable Rawlins, was superstitious, and while they were busy making the sign against evil, I was able to wriggle free.

I never saw the hole until I was through it. Now, I'm not talking about a hole in the ground or any benign hole in a wall. I'm talking about a gaping hole in reality — a rip, if you will, in the space-time continuum. I know you are going to say: "How could you not see a ragged rift of absolute darkness and horror? These holes have been around for the last twenty years, virtually your entire life." And yes, on two previous occasions I have had the misfortune to fall through such holes. But please take into account my diminished eyesight, the continued spinning of the world, and the pursuit of the angry constable.

With the proper application of magic, people have always been able to open a passage between Aracidia, my home realm, and Earth, Aracidia's technological sister realm, but it took a wizard of enormous power. For the last twenty years, however, holes have been randomly opening both here in Aracidia and on Earth, and people inadvertently crossing between realms has not been an uncommon occurrence, although believe me, it is dangerous and most unpleasant. It's estimated that one of every two people who enters a rift doesn't appear on the other side. What happens to them no one knows. Why these rifts in reality have started to occur is also a mystery. Some believe the use of nuclear weapons on Earth is responsible. Others think it was out of control, power-mad wizards here that did it. Or perhaps the two forces combined to disrupt the space-time continuum. I don't care why. I just know that falling through a hole hurt.

One minute I was barreling down the street, hoping to duck into a convenient alley and lose the constable, and the next I was having every atom in my body thrown about in ways atoms weren't supposed to be thrown. Then I was lying on my back, surrounded by a bunch of men in orange jumpsuits. Somehow I had landed straight in the middle of the Long Beach city jail. What were the odds of that happening?

I've had the misfortune to end up in Long Beach twice before. The second occasion I fell through such holes, I spent time in the jail—all because of a misunderstanding, I assure you—before I was lucky enough to find a hole in the space-time continuum to take me back to Aracidia.

"Wow, man!" one of the prisoners said. "It's that dude from Aracidia." At least I think that's what he said, my atoms still trying to resemble themselves.

I blinked and wiped the blood out of my eye. I noticed a rabbit's foot hanging from the zipper of another prisoner. As luck would have it, he also had a tattoo of a four-leaf clover on his wrist. While rabbit's feet and clovers are supposed to be signs of luck, this combination was certainly not lucky for me. You see, I recognized that tattoo. Its owner and I had had a slight misunderstanding. He seemed to be under the impression that I had stolen a gold ring he used to wear on his right hand while, I assure you, I had merely borrowed it to check the quality of the workmanship, which, actually, was very fine.

"Martin," I said, using my most charming smile. "So nice to see you again."

Martin smiled, but it wasn't a smile of friendly greeting. Instead, it was the same smile he had worn while beating me to a bloody pulp over the misunderstanding regarding the ring. I was contemplating whether Martin or Constable Rawlings was a bigger threat to me when the hole closed as abruptly as it had opened, trapping me in the prison yard. "I told you if I ever saw your face again I was going to break every bone in your body."

I stumbled to my feet and noticed that Martin was surrounded by twelve of his friends. I quickly added this up and determined that made thirteen of them. Now, as I have said, I'm not normally a superstitious man, and the number thirteen usually meant no more to me than any other number, but being outnumbered thirteen to one did seem a tad unlucky. "Ah, yes, I believe you did, but I assure you I had no intention of coming here. I didn't notice the hole."

Martin raised his eyebrows. "How could you miss seeing the hole?"

"Well . . er . . . I was kind of being chased at the time." I explained all about the cat, the street urchin, the ladder, and the constable who wanted to see me hang.

"What were you thinking?" said the tallest of Martin's friends. "Everybody knows black cats and ladders are the worst kind of luck."

Martin laughed. "Very bad luck for scrawny here." He gave me a light push in the chest.

I looked around frantically for a prison guard, the only time in my life I've desired to see a representative of the law. But the guards were on the far side of the yard and had not noticed my arrival.

Tall pulled out a sharp piece of glass, and I realized it was a piece of a broken mirror. "I say we carve up his face."

Now, as I have said, I'm not a superstitious man, but even a non-superstitious man will find his beauty marred by a broken mirror. "You said break every bone in my body. Nothing was said about carving up my face." I objected, trying to back away.

As luck would have it, the broken mirror caught the sunlight and reflected it into the eyes of another group of prisoners—a gang of the Aryan Brotherhood. I should perhaps explain that my skin is none too light. Besides, I recognized the head Brother from my prior stint in the Long Beach city jail. His name was Justin, and we too had had a misunderstanding, my having made some remark about his parentage involving a dog and a baboon.

He signaled to the other members of the Brotherhood, and they too converged on me. I counted quickly and discovered there were also thirteen of them. I racked my brain for something clever to say to avoid getting every bone in my body broken and my face carved like a pumpkin. The best I could think of was a joke about why the Nazi crossed the road that I didn't think either group would appreciate.

They stopped advancing about two feet from me. "He's ours," said Martin, staring at the head Brother.

"You can have what's left of him when we're through with him," Justin said.

I put up a hand toward each of them. "Now, ladies, no need to fight over me." This may not have been the smartest thing to say because both men stopped glaring at each other and turned their full attention to me. But at that moment, I saw a penny lying face up at my feet. Now, I'm not normally a superstitious man, and I have left many a penny lie, but today I reached for it. At that exact moment, both men swung for me, but because of the penny, I was no longer there, and they hit each other instead.

An all-out brawl erupted, and I was able to crawl free of the fray with scarcely a bruise to show for it. While I was congratulating myself on my escape, I looked down and saw the crack in the concrete directly under my feet. Not knowing who my mother was, I was not much concerned with breaking my momma's back, but I noticed the crack start to widen and realized it was not an ordinary crack, but another rift in the space-time continuum. What are the odds of encountering two on the same day?

Before I could decide whether to jump aside or allow myself to fall through it, I was sucked into the fathomless void to have my atoms thrown about again. I nearly laughed in relief when I found myself on my back on the streets of my beloved Longston Beachidea.

Then I glanced to the side and saw a pair of boots. I looked up to find that they belonged to — you guessed it — Constable Rawlings.

DOLPHINS AND SEA LIONS

Author Note: "Dolphins and Sea Lions" was originally published in *The Wifiles*, 2011. This story is a prequel to *The Goddess's Choice*, focusing on Robrek's mother and uncle Slathek.

Slathek of Mahngbhayo had been in Murtaghan, the capital of Korthlundia, nearly a month and had disposed of his cargo and come a fair way towards buying merchandise for the return trip. He sat at a table in the Clothmakers' Guild Hall, counting the gold coins carefully before pushing them across the table to the linen merchant. He knew the amount was as had been agreed upon, but he loved the way the cool coins felt against his skin and the way they gleamed in the sunlight streaming through the window. He hated to part with them, but he knew the linen he'd purchased would bring him twice this amount when he returned home. He smiled as he thought of the jewels and the art he would buy with them. He'd commission a marble statue for the entry hall of his port home — a young woman riding on the back of a dolphin. Malkekek charged outrageous prices for his work, but the sculptor was the best, and with the profit of this year's trip, Slathek could easily afford it.

"A pleasure doing business with you," Abenzio said, sweeping the coins into his purse. "Am I to see the lovely miniature of your sister again?"

Slathek tensed. "You've seen it every year for the last ten. Do you think you'll suddenly remember something you had forgotten?" Still, he pulled his copy of her miniature out from under the tunic and allowed it to be passed around the table. He'd placed the small portrait in a gold locket, studded with diamonds and sapphires. Annke, the captain of one of his three ships, said he was a fool to wear something so valuable around his neck, but Slathek had faith in the sword he wore at his side. It hadn't failed him yet.

"Such a lovely girl." Abenzio shook his head, clicking his tongue. "Your older sister, wasn't she?"

"Yes," Slathek answered, tucking the miniature back under his tunic. His mother died in childbirth, and Sphry had been like a mother to him.

The barbarian clicked his tongue again, but his eyes gleamed. "Such a shame. So much evil in the world to corrupt innocence."

Slathek's lips tightened, and his eyes narrowed. Despite the fact Slathek was half the barbarian's size, Abenzio had the sense to pale.

"I'm sorry," the barbarian stammered. "I meant no disrespect."

Slathek gathered his papers and held out his hand in the fashion of the barbarians. "I'll expect the merchandise delivered to the docks in the morning."

Abenzio shook his hand. "Yes, yes, of course."

Slathek walked back through the crowded streets of Murtaghan towards The Traveler's Haven, where he always stayed.

Among the numerous stalls lining the street, Slathek caught sight of an herb seller. He stopped and examined her wares. The scent of rosemary and comfrey filled the air, bringing him back to his childhood. Despite the fact he had no use for it, he bought a bag of dried rosemary, paying the outrageous sum the herb seller asked. He wouldn't lower himself to haggle over a few coppers. He tried to remember what Sphry had used rosemary for, and it saddened him that he couldn't. At six, he'd known the use of nearly all the herbs in his sister's stillroom and had wanted to be just like her. He wondered just what had happened to that boy and what Sphry would think of the man he'd become.

* * *

Slath had a pestle in his hand and was crushing dried burdock root into powder for his sister. It was hard work, but when they were finished, Sphry had promised to take him to the beach. Aunt Dnrill didn't think he was big enough to go by himself, and Aunt Dnrill never did anything fun. She never did anything at all, but cook and clean. He didn't like Aunt Dnrill who wasn't really his aunt, just some woman their father paid to look after him while he was away trading. Sphry claimed that now she was thirteen they didn't need Aunt Dnrill anymore, but it made their father feel less guilty about leaving them so often and for so long. Slath barely knew his father. Even when he was home, he spent most of his time at his office on the docks counting his money and buying merchandise. But Slath didn't care. He had Sphry. Sphry was a healer and took care of every hurt or sick thing. Slath wanted to be a healer just like her when he got bigger. He prayed daily to the Father and the Mother to grant him enough magic so he could. They hadn't answered yet, but there was still plenty of time. Sphry's magic hadn't become strong until she was ten, and he was only six.

The cauldron over the fire hissed as Sphry added ingredients. She looked beautiful in the firelight; even the other boys agreed his sister was the most beautiful of all their sisters. A wild fox sat calmly next to her on the counter.

"What are you making, Sphry?"

"An ointment for this poor fox, Slath. See, he's gotten into something." Sphry pointed to the side of the fox were the fur had been rubbed off, and Slathek could see the fox's skin was red and inflamed.

"How do the wild ones know to come to you?" The fox had hardly been the first wild creature to show up on their doorstep.

Sphry wrinkled her forehead. "I'm not sure. Perhaps they can sense me like I sense them. At least, the dolphins can. It's hard to ask other animals because their minds aren't complex enough."

The fox's eyes followed Sphry's every movement. Slath was immensely proud of his sister. Her medicines were the best in the harbor. Everyone said so.

* * *

Slath held his sister's hand and skipped at her side. "I'm going to build my biggest sand castle ever today. Big enough to have a thousand rooms, and I'm going to be king of it."

"We don't have a king," Sphry reminded him. "We're a republic. Adults, like daddy, vote on the laws."

Sphry had explained this to him before, like she'd taught him how to read and write. His father said he'd hire a tutor for Slath when he got back from trading this season, but Slath hoped he'd forget again like he did last season. "In my country, there's a king, and I'm going to be it."

Sphry laughed and, fortunately, didn't bore him with any more lessons about why it was wrong for one person to make all the laws.

With their shovels and buckets, Slath and Sphry made a castle as high as Slath's waist. When it was finished, Slath pointed to the bottom right corner. "This is where your stillroom will be," he told Sphry. Beside it he used shells to build a fence. "Your herb garden will be here, and there will be lots of woods behind the castle where you can gather mushrooms and such."

"I think I'd be very happy in such a castle, but are you sure you want to be king? They have an awful lot of responsibilities. You wouldn't have much time to help me grind roots."

Slath shrugged. "I'll be a king only if I don't have enough magic to be a healer like you."

"Why not be a merchant like father?"

"No!" He jumped to his feet and stamped his foot. "I'll never be like father. He doesn't care about us. He doesn't care about anything but making more and more money." He started to tell her what the other boys had said about their father, but Sphry got that dreamy look on her face.

"They're here," she said. Slath didn't have to ask who. Only the dolphins gave her that look. As she stood and walked toward the water, Slath saw a dolphin do a flip and dive back into the water. Slath laughed. They were silly creatures. When Sphry told him the stories they told her, he nearly burst his sides laughing. He hoped someday to be able to hear the stories from the dolphins themselves, like Sphry could.

* * *

"Where is your sister?" Slath's father burst into the study in the middle of yet another boring lecture from Slath's tutor on the governments in nearby countries. Robrek claimed that because trade depended on the policies of various governments, his son needed to understand everything he could about them. Slath had tried to tell his father that he didn't want to be a merchant, but Robrek never seemed to hear him. Slath no longer knew what he wanted to be. He was starting to despair about becoming a healer. Even though he was eight now, he didn't have the slightest hint of the gift. Sphry told him to be patient, but that was easy for her to say.

She was only fifteen and already the strongest healer in the port city.

"I don't know," Slath answered. He almost never got to spend time with his sister during the day anymore, except on holy days.

"She didn't go down to the beach, did she? I warned her the pirate ships had been sighted." The pirates often grabbed young girls and sold them in faraway lands. His father wouldn't tell him why they only wanted girls, but Slath figured they made the girls do the disgusting thing that his father paid women to come to the house and do with him. Sphry said that was how babies were made, so Slath decided he didn't want to be a father. The way his father groaned and the woman cried out when they did it made Slath think it hurt a lot. Sphry said she didn't know.

Robrek sent his servants to every place Sphry might have gone. Slath ran to their favorite spot on the beach. But Sphry wasn't there. The dolphins were playing off shore, and again Slath wished for enough magic to understand them. Sphry sometimes gathered things from tidal pools in the rocks at the far end of their beach, so Slath went toward them, looking and calling for her.

When he climbed on the rocks, Sphry wasn't among the tidal pools either, but then Slath saw it—Sphry's gathering basket, the basket that used to belong to their mother, his sister's most precious possession. It was lying among the rocks tipped over and trampled. "No!" he cried gathering up the broken pieces. He frantically searched the shore for her, but at the base of the rocks, he noticed a place where a boat had been pulled ashore, and he knew they'd taken Sphry and with her everything that was bright about his world.

* * *

When Slath put the broken basket on his father's desk, Robrek's face went white. He fingered the pieces as if he didn't know what the object was, then grabbed Slath and hugged him as Slath never remembered being hugged before. "We'll find her, Slathek. We'll bring her back. This I vow by the names of the Holy Mother and Father."

* * *

Slath and his father walked through the slave market in Neaseria. They had been tracing the path of the pirates for nearly three months now. His father had learned that this market was where they disposed of their goods. Slath and his father wore gloves and scarves wrapped around their heads, covering their faces like the Bendouins did. His father said that they mustn't be recognized as Mahngbhayons or the slave traders might not be as forthcoming. They passed cage after cage full of men, children, and old women of all different shades and hues — some as black as ebony and others so white Slath wondered if they were ill until Robrek told him that was the normal color of their skin. Some of the men were covered with hair, even on their faces. The eyes that looked at him from the cages were full of rage, hatred, or despair. He felt sick at the thought of his sister in a cage like that, but when they found her, they had plenty of gold to buy her and bring her back home. Then things would be like they used to be.

Ahead was a gaudy tent. Robrek said it was the last place he wanted to find his daughter, but the first place they needed to look. Sphry was beautiful. She wouldn't be sold to work some planter's fields. The tent was full of girls; they weren't in cages, but chained by the neck to posts placed throughout. They wore nothing more than two small pieces of cloth — one wrapped around their breasts and the other around their privates. Neither piece covered much.

When they went inside the tent, a huge man with ebony skin hurried up to them. "Welcome!" the man enthused. "What type of girl can I interest you in? We have samples from across the world."

Robrek matched the man's accent almost perfectly when he answered. Robrek had a knack for languages, which Slath was discovering he'd inherited. "I have seen a girl like the one I want. Creamy brown skin, black hair, emerald eyes, and small enough to fit under my arm." Slath's father went on to describe Sphry in detail as if she were one of those women he wanted to make disgusting noises with. Slath vowed to kill any man who did that to his sister.

The slave trader grunted. "Sounds like you want a Mahngbhayon. They're hard to come by. I had about a half dozen of them a month ago brought in by Salomian pirates. They're the only ones you can get Mahngbhayons from since they have a unique way of acquiring them, if you know what I mean." The man winked and nudged Robrek, and Slath wondered why his father didn't break the man's neck. "Too bad I sold the lot to traders heading for the northern countries. Apparently dark skin, but not too dark, is seen as exotic up there."

Robrek stared straight ahead like a dead man as they left the slave traders' tent. "We can't follow until spring, Slath, my lad. The seas are far too dangerous now. If only we'd found this place a month sooner."

* * *

That winter Slath's father sold his old ship and bought a larger, faster one. He learned what items of trade the cold countries coveted and filled the ship with them. Now nine, Slath insisted on new tutors who could teach him the languages of the cold countries, but most of all he insisted on a fencing master and a well-made sword. His father gave him everything he asked for. He applied himself to his studies as he never had before, and by the time for safe sailing arrived, he knew the rudiments of five new languages, and his fencing master declared him adequate with a blade.

It was a three month journey to the cold countries, and Slath continued to practice both languages and the sword throughout. He helped with any of the sailing tasks that would increase his strength or balance. His father noticed nothing of what he did, but spent his days either on deck staring at the northern seas or in his cabin staring at a miniature of Sphry that had been painted shortly before she was taken. He'd had a copy made for Slath as well, and Slath always wore it around his neck under his tunic. Slath took it out several times a day to look at his sister's face, but he didn't waste time staring at it as his father did. He got straight back to practicing his sword work or speaking to sailors who knew the languages of cold countries. He would help find his sister. Then he'd kill the men who forced her to make those disgusting noises.

Slath had the chance to practice his languages as they searched the slave markets of port after port, but he found no use for his blade that year. They'd found no sign of the slavers who purchased his sister from the Nesearian harbor and no sign of Mahngbhayon slave girls. It was years before they found the trail again.

* * *

Slath and his father walked along the docks of Murtaghan, the capital of one of the smallest of the cold countries. The people of Korthlundia had pasty white skin and looked like giant, animated corpses whose hair refused to stop growing. Slath thought them closer to animals than to humans. Now sixteen years old, Slath had grown more than adequate with his sword, and he spoke over a dozen languages of the cold countries, including the barbaric grunt of the Korthlundians.

His father's eyes, which had grown deader and deader every year they returned empty handed, grew feverishly alive as they followed the directions to the auction house which dealt illicitly in foreign whores. Slavery was illegal in

Korthlundia, but it still flourished in the underground market. From the outside, the slave auction house looked like any of the hundreds of other warehouses that fronted the harbor. Inside, nearly every surface was covered in red velvet. They found the owner—a hairy giant, missing half his teeth and with the foulest breath Slath had ever encountered. His father held out the miniature of Sphry. "It would have been nearly seven years ago."

The man laughed without taking the picture. "You think I remember every tits and ass that passes through here."

"Perhaps you remember this one." Robrek's voice was tight as he put a handful of silver coins on the man's desk.

The man leaned forward in his chair, swept the coins into his hand, and took the miniature. He smiled widely. "Oh, yes, I remember this one. Fiery temper she had. She objected to what men were doing with one of the other girls, so we had good fun with her instead."

Slath drew his sword and pointed it to the man's overlarge belly. He'd sworn he'd kill all who had her. "You're talking about my sister!"

But the auctioneer didn't even blush. "Every whore is someone's sister. Now put that toy away before you hurt yourself with it." The man spoke as if he were a child. Since Slath's people were much smaller, Korthlundians were always mistaking him for younger than he was.

His father put his hand on Slath's sword arm. "However much he deserves it, put it away, son. We're here to find Sphry, not avenge her."

"I'm here to do both." Slath glared at the auctioneer who paled as he realized Slath's size didn't coincide with his age or ability.

"Now look here, you can't condemn a man for doing his job."

"Slath, put it away. I won't see you hanged for killing such trash."

Jamie Marchant

Slath hesitated. It had never occurred to him that he might face consequences for killing his sister's debauchers. Slath sheathed his sword.

"Who bought her?" his father asked, adding a few more coins to the pile.

"I don't rightly recall," the man said. "But whatever brothel it was, she'd hardly still be there. Sailors use up whores fast."

"We'll try them all," Slath's father insisted.

* * *

Slath blanched as they went through the first brothel's front door. Girls wearing nearly nothing, many Slath's age or younger, stared at him with hollow eyes. Slath couldn't help the tightening in his groin at the sight of so much flesh.

A plump woman with large breasts hurried forward to greet them. "Welcome, sir, what can I interest you in today?" The woman's eyes widened as she caught sight of Slath. "The boy isn't for sale, is he?"

Robrek slammed the woman against the wall. "This boy is my son."

A huge man grabbed Robrek from behind and threw him out the door onto the cobblestone street. Remembering what his father said about being hanged, Slathek merely got out his miniature of Sphry and asked about her. The woman shook her head.

The next brothel wasn't as bad as the first. Three woman—one white, one brown, and one black, lounged on couches. They weren't chained, and they wore robes of a transparent fabric. Slath could see the full outline of their bodies. Slath tore his eyes away from the women, but as his father talked to the brothel owners, Slath's eyes kept drifting back to the women, running his eyes over their bodies, and wondering what it would feel like to touch one. He'd heard the sailors talking of the pleasures of a woman's body, but he'd had no chance to find out for himself.

Hours later when they finished making the rounds of all the brothels in the harbor district, Slath's groin was throbbing, and he could think of nothing but room after room of nearly naked women—any of which could be had for a few coins.

After Robrek went up to bed, Slath snuck sneaked out of the inn and back to the brothel district. He entered the one that had seemed the cleanest and where the whores had seemed the most eager to serve. He handed over the coins to the brothel owner and chose a whore as black as ebony with huge breasts and firm thighs.

* * *

Hoping his father wouldn't know where he'd been or what he'd done, Slath whistled as he walked back to the Traveler's Haven. But his father was waiting for him at one of the tables near the door. "So do you think you're a man now?" his father asked. "Do you think bedding your sister makes you one?"

Blood rushed to Slath's face. "She wasn't my sister!"

"She's somebody else's sister, somebody's daughter! Those women are little better than slaves, like your sister is!"

Slath ran from the inn. At the dock, he tore off his clothes and dove into the water of the harbor. The water was frigid, far colder than it ever got in Mahngbhayo. But not cold enough to cool his burning shame. He swam for the rock out in the harbor that the sea lions used. It was farther than he'd realized, and he was shaking with cold and exhaustion by the time he pulled himself onto it. The sea lions barked at him, but kept their distance. "Did you speak to her like the dolphins did?" he asked the beasts, but he could hear them no better than he'd been able to hear the dolphins. Only Sphry had had that magic, and he'd dishonored her. He vowed he'd never sleep with another whore. But as the sun began to rise, he realized what his father wouldn't admit. It had been seven years since Sphry was taken. His sister was dead, and the family fortunes were dwindling due to his father's obsessive search. It was time to stop looking for her and tend to other matters. If his father wouldn't, then he'd have to.

* * *

The bark of the sea lions took Slathek by surprise. He hadn't realized he'd been that close to his ships. He stopped and gazed on the three ships he now owned. While his father searched fruitlessly for Sphry, Slathek had made the family prosper, becoming a sharper trader at eighteen than his father was at forty-five. But as Slath looked at the sea lions, he realized he'd dishonored his sister far more thoroughly than that single night with the whore. Sphry was the magic of his childhood—a magic that healed and mended. He'd replaced that magic with the cold comfort of gold.

Perhaps he wouldn't commission the dolphin statue after all.

□

JENNIE'S WOLF

Author Note: "Jennie's Wolf" was originally published in *Of Dragons & Magic: Tales of Lost Worlds*. Witty Bard Publishing, 2014.

Arlene sighed as she copied Dr. Elston's final exam. As a secretary in the English Department, Arlene had lots of copying to do at the end of the semester. Like most aspects of her job, it wasn't hard work, just tedious. To entertain herself, she mimicked Rob Schneider "The Richmeister" from Saturday Night Live. "Arlene. The Arlister. The Arlinator. Making some copies."

Hester came into the room with a stack of yet more copying and raised her eyebrows at Arlene.

"Have to do something to keep myself sane," Arlene said, taking the stack.

"I'm afraid it's too late for that."

Arlene laughed uneasily and went back to copying. Although she knew Hester was joking, Arlene suspected that her fellow secretary might be right. Arlene was seeing things again. When she looked out the window at the Cal. State Long Beach campus, she kept seeing wolves skulking through the trees. She was certain they weren't really wolves. Wolves didn't belong in the heart of L.A. County. Wolves belonged in stories about Little Red Riding Hood and The Three Little Pigs.

Arlene didn't mention the wolves to Hester. She'd learned long ago to keep her hallucinations to herself.

Shaking off her insanity, Arlene continued copying. When she finally finished, she spent her time watching the clock until five p.m. crawled around. Then she grabbed her purse out of the bottom desk drawer and headed out the door as fast as she could, in hopes of catching the 5:10 bus. As she swung her purse over her shoulder, she told herself for the hundredth time that she really needed to clean it out. It seemed to weigh nearly fifty pounds, and Arlene didn't need any more weight to lug around; she was already carrying nearly a hundred extra pounds stark naked.

Telling herself that she really needed to get in shape, Arlene puffed to the bus stop. She reached it just in time. She clambered aboard the bus and found an empty seat, then opened her latest fantasy novel. Arlene loved stories about adventure and the supernatural. They helped her escape from her everyday life.

After a fifteen minute ride, Arlene got off at her stop and started down the deserted alleyway that led to her apartment. Suddenly, she stopped--into the mouth of the alley ahead of her stalked two wolves. They couldn't possibly really be there. Certain she was hallucinating, she started forward again, but a half dozen more wolves popped into sight. Hallucinating or not, Arlene decided she'd better go the long way home. She turned and started back down the alley. She heard the pads of the wolves' feet following her. Alarmed, she broke into a run. She didn't normally hear her hallucinations.

The wolves' hot breath licked the backs of her legs. This was no hallucination! If she didn't make it to the end of the alley in time, she was dinner. Please, get me, out of this alive. And I promise I'll start an exercise program. I'll join a gym, lose weight. And I mean it this time.

But whatever god she'd prayed to must not have been listening. Two of the wolves leapt past her and turned, blocking her way. Arlene stopped dead. Two wolves in front, half a dozen behind. With her purse, she took a desperate swing at the closest wolf, hitting him in the side of the head with a resounding clunk.

The wolf, a big gray one, growled, baring its teeth. Arlene backed against the alley wall and prepared to swing again. At least she'd go down fighting.

The gray wolf stopped advancing and shuddered from head to tail. All the fur melted off its body; its snout shortened; its ears moved down to the sides of its head. Arlene yelped. The wolf disappeared, a young man taking its place. A very attractive and very naked young man knelt at her feet. Slowly he straightened, completely unselfconscious about his nakedness.

This couldn't be real. Arlene squeezed closed her eyes and opened them again. She pinched herself hard, but nothing changed. She was still surrounded by seven wolves and one naked young man who, she was almost sure, used to be a wolf. It wasn't that she didn't like werewolves. She loved stories about werewolves and vampires and all sorts of supernatural creatures. But that was what they should remain—characters in stories.

"What do you have in that thing, a bowling ball?" the naked young man asked, pointing to her purse with one hand and rubbing the side of his head with the other.

"A gun," she lied, sticking her hand inside her purse. "So you and your friends had better turn right around and trot out of here."

The man crossed his arms. "You haven't got a gun."

Arlene's hand closed around a screwdriver in her purse. She'd forgotten why it was in there. She poked it against the side of her purse to mimic a gun barrel. "Go away, or I'll shoot."

The man stepped forward and grabbed Arlene's purse. They tussled. Arlene managed to keep hold of the screwdriver, but the man ended up with the purse. "I told you you didn't have a gun."

"Yeah, but I can poke your eyes out." Arlene brandished her screwdriver.

"There's no need to be afraid," the young man said. "We won't hurt you. My name's James." He tossed her purse back to her.

Arlene caught it, but nearly dropped the overweight thing. She glanced behind her, but the wolves there had all settled down on their haunches. It didn't appear as if she was about to be eaten, and James hadn't done anything threatening, except standing there naked. "If I'm really good, will you go away, and we can all pretend this never happened?"

"We need your help," James said. "We've lost a pup."

"Well, can't you just smell it out? Don't you have like a super sense of smell or something?"

"Not missing physically. Lost on the spiritual plane." James pointed behind Arlene. She turned and saw a young pup peeking out from behind one of the huge wolves, probably its mother.

"I don't understand."

James shook his head. "They're not supposed to go through the change until they reach puberty and can control it. When they change when they're that young"—he gestured toward the pup—"sometimes they become lost and can't find their way to change back. If she doesn't change back before the end of the full moon, she could become stuck that way— forever a wolf, losing all her humanity. Jennie's only three."

The little pup peeked up at Arlene. It was about the cutest thing she'd ever seen, and she wanted to gather it in her arms and give it a big hug. "That's terrible, but I don't know what you want me to do about it."

James rolled his eyes. "Isn't it obvious? Walk the spiritual plane with her and show her the way back."

Arlene put her finger in her ear to clear the wax out. She couldn't have heard correctly. "You want me to what?"

"Don't be obtuse!" James flipped a hand in frustration; Arlene knew what obtuse meant, and she didn't much like being called it. "What else would we want you to do?"

"I don't know. Fly maybe." It would have made as much sense. "I'm afraid you've got the wrong person."

James crossed his arms again and thrust his chin forward. "Don't you shamans take some kind of vow to help those in need, or are you hoarding all your magic for your own self-aggrandizement? You'd think you'd have a little of it to spare." He gestured toward her ample belly.

Arlene tried to suck in her gut. "Excuse me, 'you shamans'? Sorry to disappoint you, I'm only a secretary."

"Who do you think you're fooling? We can smell the magic dripping off you. The stench is so raw we could smell it from the beach all the way up at the university. How do you think we tracked you down?" James jerked his chin and gave Arlene a "so-there" smirk. "And you're shaped like a shaman, too. A shaman who's been hoarding her magic."

Arlene stared down at her stomach. Hoarding? Magic? Too weird. "The only thing I've been hoarding is food. Now, I'd love to help you, but I have no idea how to walk the spiritual plane. I was too young to be a hippie. Missed out on all that sort of thing."

Arlene heard a rustle behind her and turned to find a naked woman. She was in her early thirties and had a hand on the small pup. "Please, she's my only baby. You may not have done it before, but you can walk the spiritual plane. You have the magic. You can bring Jennie back to herself." The two humans and the six other wolves all nodded in a disconcertingly human-like manner. The young pup howled and frisked around her mother. The woman picked up the pup in her arms. "Please. Can't you at least try?"

Arlene chewed on her lip for a moment. "If you really think I can help."

"Good," James nodded, as if that settled everything. "We'll meet you down at the beach."

"Why the beach?"

James heaved an exasperated sigh. "To walk the spiritual plane, you have to be close to nature, don't you? Where else are we going to find nature in L.A.?"

James shimmered, and suddenly he was no longer a naked young man but a huge gray wolf. Jennie's mother did the same. Then all the wolves ghosted around her and were gone, taking the pup with them.

Arlene began walking down the alleyway. "It was a dream. There is no such thing as werewolves. I'm heading home where any sensible person would be this time of night. Maybe I'll find myself in my own bed."

But the pup's eyes haunted her, and she knew, crazy or not, she had to go to the beach. It was only six blocks away, so Arlene decided to walk rather than try to find a bus. The night was cool, but she was sweating and breathing heavily by the time she made it to the park above the beach. "I definitely have to join a gym," she said, remembering her promise. She leaned against the rail for a few moments before undertaking the long descent to the beach. In the light of the full moon shining on the water, Arlene could see the wolves milling about. If they'd been a hallucination, she was still having it. She climbed down about fifteen hundred and sixty-two steps — at least that was how many it seemed by the time she reached the sand.

More trash than nature on the beach, she huffed across the sand toward the wolves. The L.A. river emptied into the ocean at Long Beach, bringing all its filth with it, and the breakwater kept the filth from washing out to sea. Everything from used syringes to candy bar wrappers littered the beach. That, along with the bike path and artificial lights, made it seem far more a human zone than a natural one, but if the wolves said she should walk the spiritual plane at the beach, she'd walk the spiritual plane at the beach.

The big gray wolf was holding a small cooler in its mouth. The wolf set the cooler down at her feet and then shimmered to become the naked James. "It's all in there for you."

Arlene opened the cooler to find a six pack of Red Bull. She shook her head. "Oh, no. Caffeine gives me headaches."

"Of course it does if you hoard rather than share your magic." James made a gesture at Arlene's size. "Besides, all shamans know you have to drink Red Bull or smoke peyote to walk the spiritual plane, and we couldn't get ahold of any peyote."

"If you know other shamans, why aren't you asking them?"

James sighed. "Our shaman died in an accident on the 405. We were looking for a new one when the crisis came up with the pup."

Arlene looked around for the pup and saw her peeking out from behind her mother. Suddenly emboldened, the pup strutted forward and sniffed first the Red Bull and then Arlene.

Arlene nodded. "So I drink this stuff, and then what?"

"You walk the plane, of course. Bring little Jennie back," James said.

That wasn't a lot of help, but Arlene picked up one of the Red Bulls, popped the top, and settled down in the sand to drink it. The ocean waves lapping against the shore made a soothing sound. Not that they were very big waves because of the breakwater.

By the time she'd downed the first Red Bull, she was anything but soothed. The caffeine had given her the headache she'd anticipated, and her muscles twitched. By the time she'd downed the second, her heart was pounding. She got up and paced along the beach. By the time, she'd downed the third she was certain she was going to die, her heart trying to force its way through her chest. "I can't drink anymore," she insisted.

James looked down at the three remaining cans. "You have to. The magic is gathering. Can't you feel it?"

The only thing Arlene felt was a desperate need to pee.

The pup sniffed around the empty cans, and her mother shimmered and appeared as a naked woman. "Please," she said again. "You're the only one who can help Jennie. If she hasn't changed back by the time the moon sets, it will be too late."

Arlene sighed and picked up another Red Bull. She'd drunk half of it when the ocean burst into a kaleidoscope of color—reds and greens and blues, purples and oranges. She gasped and looked at the wolves. They too were shining with light, especially little Jennie. Moreover, she felt good, really good. The need to pee had disappeared and was replaced by a terrible thirst. She needed every drop in those remaining two cans. Before she realized it, they were empty.

She wanted to dance and sing. She wanted to play chase with the waves. She wanted to hug everyone in the world and tell them how much she loved them. She twirled around laughing and fell on her rump in the sand. The world tilted oddly, and when it righted itself, she saw a toddler crouching next to the wolf pup. Arlene gasped in surprise, but then she noticed that each of the wolves had a naked human crouching nearby. Somehow, she must have done it. She was walking the spiritual plane. She saw what she needed to do: grasp little Jennie's hand and lead her back through the wolf. She could do this. Her life would be worth more than filing and copying. She'd be a hero.

She reached out to Jennie. "Come with me, Jennie. I'll bring you back to your mother."

Both the wolf pup and the image of the little girl shook their heads. "No! Like wolf!"

Arlene tried to grab Jennie's hand, but the girl danced out of reach. Arlene hadn't had much experience with children. She crouched down and tried reason. "You can be a wolf next full moon. Don't you want to be a little girl, too?"

Jennie backed away, shaking her head vigorously. "Jennie like wolf! Jennie be wolf!" The wolf pup howled.

Since reason didn't seem to be working, Arlene tried to be stern. "Come here this instant! I'm taking you back to your mother." Arlene reached out.

Jennie backed away farther. Arlene decided the time for talking was over and made a grab for the child. Jennie danced out of reach. Arlene ran after her, but the soft sand made her awkward, and Jennie easily evaded her. Soon after the chase had began, Arlene was sweating profusely and gasping. She had to plop down in the sand or risk fainting. She really needed to join that gym.

Arlene looked up, and the wolves were staring at her, their shadowy humans by their side. Jennie's mother asked, "What's wrong? Where's Jennie?"

Arlene shook her head, struggling for breath. "Jennie doesn't want to come back. She likes being a wolf."

The mother let out a mournful wolf-like howl. "You have to bring her back! There isn't much time left." She pointed toward the full moon on the edge of the horizon.

"I'm open to suggestions. I can't catch her, and she won't come to me."

"Sing. Jennie likes songs."

Arlene gave Jennie's mother a "you've got to be kidding" look. "I can't sing. I sound like a wounded cow."

"Jennie won't mind."

Arlene stared at the mother a moment longer, then shrugged to herself. If they wanted singing, she'd give them singing. She tried to think of a children's song. Only one came to mind. She sang, "Old McDonald had a farm. E-I-E-I-O." The older wolves whimpered; some even covered their ears with their paws, but little Jennie perked up. So Arlene kept singing, "And on that farm he had a—"

"Wolf!" Jennie blurted, stepping a little closer.

"A wolf," Arlene sang. "E-I-E-I-O. With a howl, howl here, and a howl, howl there. Here a howl, there a howl, everywhere a howl, howl. Old McDonald had a farm. E-I-E-I-O." While Arlene sang, Jennie crept closer and closer until she was within grabbing range. Arlene took the child's hand. "Here, sit on my lap, and I'll sing some more." Jennie happily climbed into Arlene's lap. Although Arlene saw the child, she could feel the warm fur of the wolf pup. She began another chorus. "Old McDonald had a farm. E-I-E-I-O. And on that farm he had a—"

"A pig!" Jennie shouted. "Wolves eat pigs!"

"A pig," Arlene sang. "E-I-E-I-O. With an oink, oink here, and an oink, oink there. Here an oink, there an oink, everywhere an oink, oink. Old McDonald had a farm. E-I-E-I-O."

Jennie clapped. "Again! Again!"

"You sing," Arlene said.

Jennie lifted her head and tried, but all that came out was a howl.

"Oh, dear," Arlene said. "You have to change back into a human to sing. How about you change back now, and you can be a wolf later?"

Jennie jumped to her feet. "Okay!"

Arlene struggled to her feet and took the child's hand. "This way." Arlene walked with Jennie and helped her merge with the wolf pup and come out the other side again.

The wolf pup shimmered, and Jennie and the wolf traded places. Instinctively, Arlene shut her eyes and withdrew from the spiritual plane. When she opened her eyes, she was surrounded by naked people of all ages, laughing and patting her on the back. Jennie's mother was holding Jennie in her arms and crying in relief. "Thank you," she said. "Thank you for bringing my little girl back." Arlene beamed. She'd done something good. She'd never be just a secretary again.

"Everybody sing," Jennie said.

Everybody sat down in the sand, and they started another chorus of E-I-E-I-O.

☐

THE BULL RIDING WITCH

Author's Note: "The Bull Riding Witch" was originally published in *Short-Story.me*. January 2011. It was reprinted in *Urban Fantasy*. (KYStory, 2013.)

I remember little of my life before I woke up with a raging hangover and inside a body I knew wasn't mine. But you try explaining to people that you're a woman trapped in a man's body. See how far that gets you, especially when you're a bull rider.

I have a rodeo in Lafayette tonight, so I'm trying to get ready. Not an easy feat if you've ever seen my trailer. I find my western shirt and jeans easily enough, but my belt is buried somewhere in the goddess awful mess. You'd think with its huge buckle I could find it, but everything that isn't covered by frozen pizza boxes and empty beer cans is stacked two feet to three feet high with books—Jim Butcher, Barbara Hambly, Mercedes Lackey, Parallel Universes, Guide to the Supernatural for Dummies. Unfortunately, the books have proven about as useful as the pizza boxes in explaining what happened to me. But somebody, somewhere has to be able to tell me how I got stuck in Josh Killenyen's body and, more importantly, how to get back into my own.

There is a knock on my trailer door, and I open it. Mr. McGillihan is standing there. In exchange for odd jobs, Uncle Gilly — as everyone calls him, although to my knowledge he's nobody's uncle — lets me keep my trailer on his land and pays me a pittance. About enough to keep the insurance current on my truck. Insurance for myself is impossibly expensive since my profession tends to include a lot of injuries.

"Horse. Colic." Uncle Gilly nods toward the barn. He rarely speaks an entire sentence.

I follow Uncle Gilly into the nearby barn. When I enter, I feel a crushing pain in my gut. Wild Girl is rolling her eyes, snorting and groaning. Her gut feels just like mine, and let me tell you, it isn't pleasant. Colic is one of the most painful and dangerous things that can happen to a horse. I approach carefully because a colicky horse doesn't pay much attention to its surroundings and can step on you without even realizing you're there. I touch her, and she instantly calms. I kneel next to her and put my hands on her gut. I close my eyes and reach inside Wild Girl's intestines with my magic. They're blocked all right. Uncle Gilly must have bought a finer grade of grain because it's packed her insides up tight. I work on loosening it up and moving it along the intestines. Wild Girl lets out an immense fart and then poops out a huge pile of . . . well, you know.

I straighten, both my guts and Wild Girl's feeling a ton better. "She's fine now, Boss," I tell Uncle Gilly.

"Good." He nods and walks away. Neither of us has ever said the word aloud, but Uncle Gilly knows about my magic. He figured it out about a year ago when one of the barn cats got hit by his truck. Nothing human could've saved the poor thing, but I did. Ever since then, he comes to me every time one of his animals has a problem. With all I save him in vet bills, you'd think he could pay me a little more.

It's probably because of my magic that someone didn't want me around, and they could hardly have picked a bigger loser to put me inside. At twenty-three Josh has never had a job, except occasional farm work and bull riding. Good thing he was decent at it, and I'm better than he was.

As I clean up after Wild Girl, I try for the thousandth time to think who might have done this to me, but I can't even remember my own name. I do remember that things are different where I come from. There are no trucks or computers or electric can openers. But magic and magical creatures—like dragons and trolls—are common. I think it's one of these parallel realms things that Hamby and some of the others write about, except they got it wrong. According to their theories, my magic shouldn't work in this world, but it does. I got the skills of my own body and Josh's as well. I didn't need to learn how to drive a truck or read, write, and speak English. Most of Josh's memories came with his body, too, but few of my own. Does Josh have my magic in my body? Have my enemies completely eliminated him, and I have no body to go back to? Being stuck inside Josh Killenyen forever isn't a pleasant thought.

I go back to my trailer and finally find my belt under Dragon Riders of Pern and Spells for the Clueless and Inept. I grab my new hat, which I bought with last week's prize money. Cost me pretty near all of it, but a proper cowboy needs a proper hat. Sometimes I find myself thinking like Josh Killenyen, and it scares me.

I get in my truck with its camper shell on back and start the three-hour drive from Hamilton on the west side of Alabama to Lafayette on the east. I'll sleep in the back tonight like I usually do for the two-day rodeos; I can't afford the price of a motel.

* * *

At the rodeo grounds in Lafayette, I drink in the scents of roasting corn, chicken-on-a-stick, and cotton candy. It's exhilarating because it means shortly I'll be having a brief, but wild ride. Nothing compares to the adrenaline rush of being on the back of a bucking bull. I wonder if in my other body I was addicted to adrenaline or if that came with Josh's body as well. On my way to the arena, I pass a booth that sells T-shirts. I spot one that says, "Cowboys make bad lovers. They think 8-seconds is a long ride." I laugh. Whoever wrote that has never been on the back of a bucking bull. Eight seconds is a long ride.

When I get to the staging area, I check what bull Josh has drawn—Man Killer. I smile; Man Killer is about the fiercest bucker on the circuit, and if I'm going to win tonight, I need a good bull. After all, half my score is based on just how hard a time the bull gives me.

From the staging area, I watch the rodeo. Fortunately, I came late enough that I missed the girls riding around with their flags to the sound of patriotic music while the announcer talks about God, America, and Dodge trucks. Rodeo people seem to worship all three with equal reverence. While I watch, I attune myself to my magic so I can be ready to ride.

Finally, it's time for the bull riding. I climb onto the launch chute, then onto Man Killer's back. He snorts, and I don't try to calm him. That was the mistake I made when I first became Josh. Instead, I reach into him until I become one with the bull, making it possible for me to match all the bull's movements like I was born on the back of a bucking bull.

I nod, and the chute opens. Man Killer roars into the arena. We're giving them quite a show when something hits my hand and I suddenly let go. I fly off and hit the ground, knocking the wind out of me. The bull's hoofs crash down inches from my head before the rodeo clowns are able to distract the beast. I run for the fence, vault over it, and stand there panting.

"What happened, man?" Dan, the closest thing to a friend Josh has, asks.

"I don't know." I shake my head, but I do know. Someone just used magic to try and kill me. I turn every which way looking for the witch, but of course, there's no one wearing a pointy black hat. I close my eyes and reach out with my magic, and I feel something, across the arena in the third set of bleachers. I tear off. Halfway there I come to my senses and stop. Charging down an unknown witch wouldn't be the brightest thing Josh ever did. Before I can decide what to do, I lose the witch's scent. I close my eyes to try to pick it up again, but I feel nothing. Still, I wait, and I only go into the back of my truck when the lights have been turned off and nobody's wandering around.

When I curl up in my sleeping bag, I start shaking. I see again the bull's hoofs coming down inches from my head. I feel the ground tremble underneath with the impact. I'm damned lucky to be alive. I don't know if I dare ride tomorrow, but if I don't, I'll barely have gas money to get back to Hamilton, and I'll have to beg Uncle Gilly for an advance on my wages to buy groceries.

What little sleep I get that night is full of dreams that nearly make me vomit. You picture the effect an 1800-pound bull would have on the human head. Not pretty, is it?

* * *

I spend all the next day prowling the rodeo grounds. I haven't a clue what I'm searching for, and I don't find any neon sign that says, "Witch will sit here tonight." When the gates open, I stand near them with my eyes closed, trying to sense everyone who comes in. The sensations of that many minds about causes me to lose what few marbles the fall yesterday didn't knock out of me, but I don't sense any magic.

When it's time for the bull riding, I decide to chance it. I really need the money, but tonight I've drawn a bull named He-man—you know, from that stupid Masters of the Universe cartoon—but he should probably be named Daisy-Muncher. I haven't a chance to win on that bull unless everybody else falls off. Dan Foster scores an eighty-three, and Ben Walker, a man I can't stand, scores an eighty-five and ends up with top prize money of eight hundred and seventy-five dollars. Nothing weird happens when I ride, but I score a whopping sixty-five and end with a whole sixty-six dollars in prize money. I guess I'll live on ramen noodles for the next week. You can survive on that, but a man ought to have meat.

I freeze. I just thought of myself as a man again. Am I completely losing touch with who I am? I almost want to cry, but then I remember men don't cry.

After a week on ramen noodles, I'm so mad I want to beat the living you-know-what out of the witch who made me lose. You might think that nearly dying should have aggravated me more than eating noodles, and yes, I still have nightmares about that bull's hoofs. But I'm hungry for something different to eat. I'm nervous as hell about the upcoming rodeo in Robertsdale, down by Mobile, and that makes me mad, too. I nurse the anger all during the five-and-a-half hour drive, fantasizing about what I'll do to the witch when I find her.

I win the bull riding in Friday night's rodeo for a whopping $615. Robertsdale's purse has always been a little on the small side. More importantly, nothing funny happens. Dan and me and some of the others go to celebrate at a sleazy bar called Hole in the Wall. The bar owner knows me and cashes my prize check. I open my fool mouth and say the first round's on me.

I pack away more than a couple of beers, then in walks Ben Walker—did I mention I can't stand him?—with a blonde wearing a ponytail, a short skirt, and a low-cut blouse. She's hanging all over Ben. The skirt and blouse don't catch my attention—although they do catch the attention of every man in the place—but what comes with her does—the distinctive odor of magic. It was her. The witch who tried to kill me.

Mad and drunk, I storm right up to the blonde, grab her arm, and shout, "Why in the hell did you try to kill me?"

Ben tells me to get my filthy hands off his woman, and I tell him where he can stuff it and his mother. He punches me in the gut. Now, Josh is big, but he must never have learned how to fight worth a hill of beans.

When I can't get up any more, Ben grabs the witch's hand. "Come on, Eileen. They let any old trash drink in this place."

* * *

I have no idea how I end up back at the rodeo grounds in the back of my truck, but I hope I didn't drive. I have a whole $75 in my pocket and a note that the bar owner took the rest to pay for damages. Why should I have to pay? It isn't like I wanted my head to break the bar stool.

The next day I'm in no condition to ride, and Ben wins the top prize money again, which pisses me off even more. Eileen isn't in the staging area like some riders' women, and I can't sense her anywhere else in the arena. But the pain in my gut is taking most of my attention, and she could be ten feet from me and I might not feel her.

* * *

Because of my magic, I heal fast, so by Tuesday I'm feeling mostly alive. I'm more than determined to find this Eileen and get the truth out of her by any means necessary. Ben is from Auburn. Thinks he's all high and mighty because he goes to the university there, and I figure Eileen is some sorority chick. So I go to the Hamilton public library where they've got computers, and I google Ben to get his address. I borrow Uncle Gilly's truck because Ben knows mine, and no, I don't ask, but I leave a note and the extra key to my truck. That should be enough for any reasonable person, especially considering how much I save him in vet bills.

I get to Ben's apartment complex at about three in the afternoon. He comes home about four with one of those university-student book bags, wearing khakis and a polo shirt. He isn't even wearing boots. Some cowboy.

About an hour later he comes back out and gets in his truck. At least he has a truck and not some fancy-assed BMW. I follow him, and as I hope, he drives over to another apartment complex and picks up Eileen. Now that I know where she lives, I lean back in Uncle Gilly's truck and wait.

About two hours later Ben's truck squeals into the lot. Eileen flings the door open almost before the truck has a chance to stop. She jumps out and screams, "I hope I never see you again," then slams the door and stalks off to her apartment. Ben squeals out of the parking lot. I can't help smiling. Anything that makes Ben unhappy is mighty fine with me.

I give Eileen a minute to get settled. Then I knock, and she opens the door. Before she can recognize me, I push my way in and grab her arm. I'm about to ask her again why she tried to kill me when I'm hit with what feels like a sledge hammer.

When I wake up, I'm on the floor with my hands and feet tied. Eileen's sitting on the couch across from me. I'm starting not to like Eileen. Now, you might be wondering why I don't magic my way out of the rope. My magic only affects living things, and even with living things, I have to be touching them, so I'm pretty much stuck. You might also be wondering why I didn't use magic on Ben the other night. Well, I was so mad and drunk I didn't think about it.

I try to stall Eileen while I work at untying the ropes. "You have me where you want me. Before you kill me could you at least tell me why?"

She snorts. "What witch would ever dare kill? Don't you know that whatever magic of ill-intent we do comes back on us four-fold? A death curse is suicide for a witch."

I have to keep her talking because I'm not having any luck with the ropes. "You expect me to believe there is another witch around here?"

She rolls her eyes like I'm the stupidest dumb ass she's ever had the misfortune to meet. "Of course there are other witches. My coven has five members, but I promise you it wasn't one of them. If it was a witch, she would need something of yours — hair, fingernail clippings, blood — to work any magic against you."

"Huh?" I know, brilliant comeback, but my head is reeling. "If you have a whole coven, how come I've never run into any of you?"

Eileen rolls her eyes again. "We don't exactly advertise. Alabama isn't friendly to witches. You know, Exodus 22:18: 'Thou shalt not suffer a witch to live.'"

I have to admit she has a point. I don't "exactly advertise" my skills either. "Well, how many witches are there around here?"

She shrugs. "Probably less than a dozen, but there might be more. The more powerful ones can shield themselves so I can't feel them. I can feel you though, but I don't know what you are."

Maybe I'm stupid, but I believe her when she says she didn't try to kill me. Mostly because if she wanted me dead, I'd be dead by now, so I decide to tell her the truth. "I'm a witch. I heal things, make them better." Well, truth be told, I can make them worse, too.

"A witch?" she says like I'm speaking Chinese. "Men aren't witches."

"I'm not a man. I'm a woman trapped in a man's body." She looks at me like I'm crazy. "Look, can you untie me? I'll tell you everything." I've just about given up getting the ropes off.

"I'm waiting for the rest of my coven. When they get here, you'll tell us everything, then we'll decide whether to untie you or kill you."

"I thought you said witches don't kill."

"If we do it as a coven, the feedback is diffused enough that we can handle it. It isn't pleasant though."

I gulp, wondering just how many times her coven has killed people, and start working harder on the ropes. Eileen just sits there with her arms and legs crossed, swinging her foot and not looking at me. "You mad at me or Ben?" I ask, hoping her fight with Ben doesn't get me killed.

"Don't mention that jerk to me!" She snorts. "Can you believe he thinks I'm a liar? He doesn't believe I'm a witch."

"You told him?"

She glares at me. "Long story. None of your business."

She looks away from me and doesn't say another word until her coven shows up. The first to arrive is a pretty black woman with her hair shaved to a fine buzz. Eileen introduces her as Kinyisha. The other three eventually arrive. Sandy, Nadeen, and Susan are white, but only Eileen has that sorority chick look.

My hands are numb, and I wonder how I'm going to talk them out of killing me. I tell them about the attack and everything I know about my situation, which isn't much. I think I'm a princess from some parallel realm. Then one day I wake up in Josh Killenyen's body. I don't know how I got here or how to get back where I belong.

When I finish, the witches sit there and look at each other for a while and then down at me and then back at each other. "I think he may be crazy," Kinyisha says. "But I don't think he's dangerous to us."

They debate my sanity for what feels like forever, and when I try to hurry them up, they threaten to gag me. Apparently, they don't have a leader, so they have to come to a consensus before they do anything. Eventually, they reach the consensus that I'm either insane or a — I won't say the word they use, but it's foul — liar. I can't convince them otherwise, especially since I can provide so few details and merely say, "I don't remember" to most of their questions.

Finally, they decide I'm probably not dangerous and untie me, but they make me stay out of touching distance. Then they debate whether or not to help me. Kinyisha — I'm starting to like her — is all for helping me. "Isn't that the purpose of a coven? To help those in need?"

"But he's nuts!" says Nadeen. "He claims he's a princess from a parallel universe. You ever hear of any parallel universes? Does he look like a princess?" I'm starting not to like Nadeen.

Still, they eventually decide that if there is some unknown witch working hostile magic in their territory, they need to know more about it. They agree that one of them should stick with me at every rodeo. Eileen doesn't want any part of it because she's mad at Ben and doesn't want to be anywhere near him. When the other women ask her why, she won't tell them anything. I figure she probably isn't supposed to tell people she's a witch. The other four agree to take turns, but Nadeen is far from happy.

* * *

Kinyisha comes with me to the next rodeo in Poplarville, Mississippi. She weaves some of my hair into a ring and charms it. She says it will block any curse aimed at my hand unless it's thrown by a really powerful witch.

After making my ring, Kinyisha sits in the stands to try to feel for the presence of any witches. Nothing funny happens, and I score an eighty-five, which means that unless somebody gets real lucky tomorrow, I'll walk off with the top prize money.

I offer to let Kinyisha sleep in the back of my truck with me.

She's reluctant, but doesn't want to pay for a motel room, and I don't have the money for one. "If you try anything, I'll curse your genitals" — she used a different word here — "and make them fall off."

"Hey, I may look like a man, but I'm a woman. I'm not interested in you that way."

She snorts, still thinking I'm crazy, but she climbs in the back with me and seems disappointed in the morning that I didn't at least try to molest her.

Nobody uses magic against me on Saturday either, and nobody tops my score. I end up with $852 in prize money.

* * *

Nothing happens over the next few weeks, and I continue to win. The witches are starting to get tired of me, and frankly, I'm tired of them, especially Nadeen who always looks at me like some garbage she just stepped in. Meanwhile, Eileen makes up with Ben — apparently he apologized and bought her flowers and chocolates and who knows what else. She talks about how wonderful he is, and I just about lose my lunch on her sorority girl shoes. She comes with me — well, with Ben — to the rodeo in Millbrook, Alabama, just up the road from Montgomery. She makes me a ring like all of the other witches have done, and I get on my bull. It's Man Killer again. We barely get out of the chute when something hits my hand, and I go flying off into the wall, breaking my arm. I'm in so much pain I can't concentrate enough to look for witches. To my humiliation, I have to be taken away in the ambulance, and, of course, with me out of it, Ben wins the top prize money.

* * *

On Saturday I drive to Auburn to meet with the witches. Eileen says she didn't feel anything, which scares the witches because only someone powerful could hide from them. Besides, Eileen's ring should have stopped anything done by a less powerful witch. They wonder if they're in over their heads and should take it to someone more powerful. They decide not to because they don't trust the powerful and because it could be one of them behind it. Instead, the witches decide they're all going to go to the next rodeo I'm fit to ride in.

* * *

I haven't a clue how I'm going to pay the hospital bill, especially since my broken arm keeps me out of bull riding for a week, but as I said, I heal a lot faster than normal, so I'm ready to ride the week after that down in Panama City, Florida. The witches are excited because they can go to the beach between rodeos. At the rodeo ground, the witches spread out throughout the crowd to feel for witches. Nothing happens on Friday night, but I draw He-man again and only score in the sixties. Ben scores an eighty-two, which will be hard to beat on Saturday night.

Eileen goes off with Ben the next day, but I go with the rest of the witches to the beach. Nadeen seems disappointed that I don't react to her in a bikini.

* * *

On Saturday I draw Kracken—he's not quite as tough as Man Killer, but mighty close, and with all of the witches spread throughout the crowd I figure I'm safe enough. I'm not about to let Ben beat me again. I ride first, and for the first few seconds, I think everything's going to be fine. Then the curse hits my hand, and I go flying off. This time when I hit the ground, I'm so mad that I don't go over the closest fence like I'm supposed to. Instead, I ignore the danger of the bull and charge across the arena to the stands where I felt the curse coming from.

I gape in disbelief. Right in the middle of the stands sits Eileen. Kinyisha and the other three witches run up to me, and they gape at Eileen, too. When the crowd clears out, Eileen claims she didn't do anything, and there must have been some other witch near her. The other witches don't believe her, and I don't either. They decide to take her off to a coven thing. I insist on coming with them, but the witches won't have any outsider involved.

"Just try and stop me from coming," I say, and Kinyisha hits me with one of those sledgehammers.

When I wake up, the witches are nowhere in sight. I go wait at my truck.

* * *

I fall asleep waiting, and about three in the morning, Kinyisha crawls in the back with me. From the sound of her voice, I can tell she's been crying. "She finally admitted it. Breaking all our codes, she sent the curse against you. Ben provided her a few strands of your hair the first time. And you gave her plenty to use the other two times. If it helps any, she wasn't trying to kill you, just make you fall off so Ben could win. She said you were using magic to win, and that wasn't fair."

"Well . . ." I start to defend myself, but I think she might have a point. I'm not about to admit it, though. Instead, I say, "So Ben believes she's a witch."

"She broke our vow of secrecy and told him. He didn't believe her at first and just gave her your hair as a joke. He made fun of her when she told him that she made you fall off the bull. That's why she was mad at him, but when you started winning again, he made up with her. She told him it was too dangerous for her to do it tonight with the rest of us here, but he bullied her into it, saying he needed the prize money for tuition."

"Whether she meant to kill me or not, she came damn close. Just what do you plan to do about that?"

"She'll be taken care of. You won't have to worry about her again."

"Taken care of? Just what does that mean?"

Kinyisha shakes her head, and no matter how many times I ask her, she won't tell me. She does offer to introduce me to the more powerful witches she knows to see if any of them can help me with my body switching problem, even though I think she still believes I'm crazy.

I take her up on her offer. Maybe something good will come out of nearly having my head smashed open like a watermelon.

THE GODDESS'S CHOICE (SAMPLE)

By Jamie Marchant

Author's Note: *The Goddess's Choice* was published by Reliquary Press in April, 2012. It is available from Amazon.com and other online book sellers. Autographed copies may be purchased directly from the author at www.jamie-marchant.com.

PART I

Chapter 1

"Please, no!" Robbie Angusstamm screamed as his father's heavy strap came whistling down on his bare back. He tried to yank his hands free, but his brother Boyden held them tightly against the dining room table. *Sulis curse it! Why do I have to be such a worthless weakling?* He promised himself he wouldn't scream again, but he screamed just as loudly the next time the strap hit.

"Sleeping by the river in the middle of the goddess-cursed afternoon! How many times must I beat you before you learn responsibility, boy?" His father brought the strap down even harder.

"I didn't mean to!" But Robbie's explanation turned into screams of pain as the strap landed again and again.

Robbie let out a humiliating whimper when his father finally stepped away and Boyden let go of his wrists. Robbie clutched a chair for support and struggled to hold back his tears. *By the goddess, don't let them see me cry.*

His father towered over him, red-faced and scowling. "Learned your lesson, boy?"

"Yes, sir," Robbie said, ashamed of how pathetic he sounded.

"I'm not going to have to send your brother looking for you again, am I, boy?" Angus Camlinstamm loomed over Robbie, making him feel even shorter than he was.

"No, sir."

"All right, then. Stop lazing around like a fool and get your chores done." Angus hung the strap on its peg by the door. "If you finish before dinner's over, I may consider letting you join us."

Like that will ever happen! Robbie clutched at his empty stomach, knowing he'd get nothing to eat before breakfast. He pulled his shirt carefully over the welts on his back and stumbled toward the back door.

As he passed through the kitchen, one of the servants quickly drew the star of Sulis in the air to ward off his evil. He hated it when people did that, but how could he blame them? He caught his reflection in the shiny pots that hung from the kitchen wall. Dark black hair, the color of night and demons. Green eyes, unlike those of the children of the goddess. Skin, darker than natural. He was also so short his brother called him a worm.

Robbie stepped outside and drew two large buckets of water from the well. He staggered toward the barn, the weight of the buckets bending him forward and pressing his shirt against his back. Praying none of the servants or farmhands would see him, he set the buckets down and emptied some of the water. His father would beat him again if he knew, and Boyden would laugh at his weakness. Boyden could carry hundred-pound sacks of grain as if they contained feathers. Boyden was everything their father wanted in a son.

Boyden hadn't killed their mother.

When he reached the barn door, he shouted for Allyn or Darien to open it, but no one came. The two farmhands were supposed to help him with the animals, but this wouldn't be the first time they'd used Robbie getting in trouble as an excuse for taking the night off. They knew he wouldn't risk another beating by telling on them.

Robbie sat the buckets down to open the door. The barn was large, with plenty of room for the dozen cows, ten horses, and four mules as well as for the large pig and her half-dozen piglets. When he entered, the cows mooed happily. The horses and mules neighed and stomped their feet in greeting. A bird whose wing he'd mended flew down from the rafters and landed on his shoulder. It nibbled his ear affectionately. The animals' joy seeped into his body like a warm, living current, strengthening him against both exhaustion and pain. Animals couldn't sense the evilness in his soul. Only here was he loved.

The animals' welcome quickly turned to cries of thirst. He cursed himself for making them wait so long for water. He hadn't meant to fall asleep by the river, but he'd been up most of the night helping a neighbor's goat with a difficult birth. "It will be alright. Robbie's here now. Just be patient, and I'll get water for all of you." The animals all quieted. They knew they could depend on him.

It took several more trips to the well to get enough water, and by the time he'd finished, his head was swimming. But he was far from finished.

He started in on the milking, and the large, gray-striped barn cat twined around his legs, mewing for attention. "Hello, Ronan. Taking care of the mice and rats for me?"

:Of course.: Ronan licked his paws as if getting the last taste of a recent kill. *:Good hunting.:* Robbie didn't exactly hear Ronan's words; it was more that he got an image or feeling from the cat's mind. He didn't know why he could understand animals; he'd always been able to. Perhaps it was another sign of his demon blood.

Robbie placed the milk in the icehouse. He then turned to cleaning the stalls and feeding the animals. When he entered Wild Thing's stall, the mare neighed. *:Wild Thing stomp father bully to mash.:* Robbie hugged his horse around the neck.

With Wild Thing, communication had always been particularly strong, and her mind seemed much more complex than other animals'. He supposed this was because Wild Thing wasn't a normal horse. Four years ago he'd found the days-old foal out on the plains, near the body of her dead mother. She'd been half-mad with hunger and fear. Her brilliant coloring, somewhere between chestnut and auburn, and the stars on her chest and forehead made it obvious she was a Horsetad. The herd of wild horses roamed free on the plains of Lundia, and people said they could never be tamed. The origin of the Horsetads was highly debated. Ages ago, some said, Sulis herself had ridden her chariot in the land, and her horses had mixed with those of earthly origin. Others said the Horsetads had escaped from the seven hells and their demon masters and were forever unwilling to allow anyone to master them again.

Robbie rubbed his face against her, choking back a sob. "Wild Thing, girl, why can't I do anything right? Why did I have to be born evil?"

Wild Thing stomped her hoof. :Not evil. Robbie good.:

Robbie knew she was wrong, but he didn't argue. Wild Thing might well be a demon herself. Many in the Valley thought so.

It was very late when he finally stumbled up to bed. Despite his hunger and the pain in his back, he was so tired he fell almost immediately asleep.

* * *

Early in the morning, Robbie stirred. When he tried to sit up, his back protested. But he knew the pain wouldn't last too long. His demon blood made him heal more quickly than normal people. He struggled to his feet and carefully got dressed. He brushed the tangles from his long, curly hair and tied it back with a strip of leather. He felt the smoothness of his face, wondering if he'd ever grow a beard. At sixteen, a lot of boys had at least some hair on their faces. Then again, he'd never heard of a demon with a beard.

As he left his room, the pain of an injured animal pressed against his mind. He hurried outside and heard a faint mewing. He followed the sound around to the back of the barn and found Ronan covered in blood. Robbie knelt beside the cat and stroked his head. "What happened to you, boy? Don't worry, Robbie's here." Robbie cradled the cat in his arms and carried him inside the barn where he kept his medicines.

As Robbie examined the injury, he sighed in relief. "It's not as bad as I thought, my boy. Some of this blood isn't yours. Got a few licks in yourself, did you?" Ronan mewed feebly, and Robbie saw an image of Ronan fighting several overgrown rats. Robbie cleaned the wound carefully. Then he treated it with one of his salves. Robbie couldn't explain how he knew how to make his remedies. No one had taught him. Certain plants just seemed to make good medicines, and certain medicines felt as if they'd help a particular problem.

As he rubbed in the salve, a trickle of energy moved through his fingers into Ronan. The sensation resembled other men's descriptions of the pleasure to be found with a woman. Ronan's wound began to heal. *Holy Sulis, what is this I do? If being a demon feels this good, maybe I shouldn't mind being one!*

By the time Robbie finished bandaging the wound, Ronan had drifted into a peaceful sleep.

* * *

After completing the morning chores, Robbie found his father outside the barn talking to Cullen Bevinstamm, a neighboring farmer. "Angus, you know all my money's gone into seed, but I'll pay you a tetra at harvest."

Angus scowled. "How do you know you'll even have a harvest? Do you have any of your wife's preserves left?" Cullen's wife was rumored to make the best preserves in the Valley, not that Robbie had ever tasted any.

The man nodded, glancing nervously at Robbie. "Yes, I think there are four or five jars."

"Send all you have back with the boy, and I'll wait for the money." Robbie's father stomped back to the farmhouse without even looking at him.

Cullen licked his lips nervously, and Robbie looked down at his feet, feeling both angry and ashamed. He hated it when people were scared of him, but he knew they had reason to be. "You have a sick animal?" he asked, still not meeting the man's eyes.

Cullen backed farther away as he explained what was wrong with his plow horse. It sounded like the lung sickness. Robbie fetched his supplies and saddled Wild Thing.

On the ride to his farm, Cullen stayed far away from Robbie and said nothing. Robbie tried not to mind. Farmers came to him because he was far better at treating animals than anyone else in the Valley, but Robbie knew they wished they had another choice.

When they neared the farm, Cullen rode a little closer. "Just so you know, I've sent my wife and children to her sister's for the day."

Just what do you think I'd do to them? I'd never hurt a woman or a child. I'd never hurt anybody. But even as he thought it, he knew it was a lie. Couldn't his demon blood cause harm even if he didn't mean it to? It had killed his own mother.

They dismounted in front of Cullen's small stable. The farmer led him inside, still careful to keep his distance. As soon as Robbie entered, his lungs tightened, making it difficult to breathe. A bay gelding coughed and wheezed. Robbie touched the horse to be sure of the extent of the illness. "He has the lung sickness, like I thought," Robbie said.

He had the man light a brazier, and he set about brewing a remedy for the horse. "I'll give this to him now, but he'll need the dose repeated three times a day for a week. Come fetch me again if he's not acting better in a day or so." As he put herbs of differing amounts into the mixture, he explained the process to the farmer.

"Sounds a bit complicated," Cullen said. "I'll fetch you some paper and ink, and you can write it down."

"I have better things to do than writing down remedies," Robbie snapped. He wasn't about to admit he was too stupid to either read or write. Father Gildas hadn't allowed him to attend the temple school, claiming the knowledge of the goddess shouldn't be shared with the seed of demons.

* * *

Just after noon, Robbie started back to his father's farm with three jars of strawberry and two jars of peach preserves in his saddlebags. He felt lightheaded, and his stomach ached with hunger. Cullen hadn't offered him so much as a piece of bread, and because of Ronan, he'd missed breakfast. By the time he reached home, the noon meal would be over.

As he took a shortcut through the woods, he got out one of the jars of preserves. "My girl, do you think my father would ever know there were five jars instead of four?"

Wild Thing's ears flicked in answer. :*Robbie hungry. Wild Thing hungry. Nice grass there. Nice jar thing here.*:

Robbie knew Wild Thing was suggesting they stop at the abandoned stable up ahead. He'd found this stable when he was twelve, during one of his wanderings through the woods looking for plants for his remedies. The stable consisted of a small barn with four stalls and a fenced-in paddock with grass for grazing. A small stream ran alongside it, and it had been in surprisingly good condition for an abandoned structure. He'd fixed it up to use as a private retreat. He stopped beside the stream and opened the jar and reveled in the sticky sweetness of the fruit; it was the best preserves he'd ever tasted. He made sure to wash any sign of the preserves from his hands and face before heading home.

* * *

In Robbie's dreams that night, the demon lady came to him. He'd dreamed of her for as long as he could remember. She always dressed in brightly colored, loose-fitting clothing; tonight she wore scarlet, trimmed with bright silver braid. Like him, the lady had black hair, green eyes, and dark skin.

As a child he'd longed for sleep, where he could curl up in her arms and listen to her stories and songs. But as he'd gotten older, the dreams had begun to trouble him. If demons loved him, didn't it mean he was as evil as people said he was?

Tonight she approached through a fog of mist, sunlight forming a halo around her. She gathered him in her arms. "I love you. You won't always be alone."

CHAPTER 2

The Princess Samantha sat at her dressing table and glowered at her reflection as her maids dressed her hair. She detested balls and loathed the hundreds of suitors who flocked around her, spouting empty flattery: "I have never seen a lovelier flower, Your Highness!" or "Your eyes rival the brilliance of the stars, Your Highness!" *If I hear that one again, I'll vomit. It wouldn't be quite so bad if even one of them meant it.* Sometimes she wished . . . . She pushed the thought away. She was the heir to the throne. She couldn't expect romance.

"Let us be painting your face tonight, Your Highness!" Ardra begged, in her north Korthian accent. Samantha's maid was as small and slight as the princess herself and had hair so blonde it was almost white.

"Yes, Your Highness," Malvina chimed in. "Lady Shela's maids said just yesterday we couldn't possibly know our business 'cause you never wear paint." Malvina, more of a typical Korthlundian woman, was tall and broad and not nearly as pretty as Ardra.

"Lady Shela," Samantha snorted in disgust. Shela wore so much paint she resembled some ghastly sea creature. Samantha knew she wasn't pretty, but she was fond of the freckles that speckled her nose and thought the emerald green brilliance of her gown set off her white skin and auburn hair beautifully. Besides being appallingly uncomfortable, paint would absolutely spoil the effect. The princess gestured toward the huge portrait that covered one wall of her bedchamber. "Do you think Danu wore paint?"

Malvina shrugged. "The Princess Danu was said to be a powerful sorceress, Your Highness. She probably didn't need to wear paint to attract men."

Samantha laughed bitterly, as she thought of the army of men waiting below. "I wish not wearing paint was all it took to scare them off. They say Danu never married, and see how happy she is."

Samantha yearned for Danu's freedom. The long-dead princess was laughing as she galloped across the fields. Danu's auburn hair flew out behind her in the wind. The stars on the forehead and chest of her horse shone against its gorgeous coat. Samantha loved this painting, which was just as well because it was bolted to the wall and couldn't be removed without tearing her chambers apart. She'd decorated the rest of her bedroom to match. Tapestries of horses covered the walls. Her dressing table, armoire, and large four-poster bed had horses carved into the woodwork. A quilt, embroidered with horses and stars, was spread over the bed. The mantle over her fireplace sported figurines of horses in gold, silver, jade, crystal, and precious stones. Every new ambassador added to her collection.

"Your Highness, you'll be having to marry one of them eventually," Ardra persisted. "The king won't be letting you hold out forever. You are seventeen, after all. Your mother was only thirteen when she married the king."

"You needn't remind me, Ardra." Samantha picked up her silver-backed brush from the dressing table. The gift from the Neasarian ambassador was inlaid with an amber Horsetad; diamonds marked the stars at its forehead and chest. She fingered it lovingly. "Do you think it's true Danu rode a Horsetad?"

"So the bards sing of her," Ardra said.

Malvina made an impatient noise in her throat. "And they also sing her kiss turned suitors into toads! You don't really believe such nonsense, do you, Your Highness? Nobody can tame a Horsetad."

"No, I suppose not," the princess sighed wistfully, then smiled at the toads that hopped around the feet of Danu's horse. *How I wish my kiss could do that!*

Finally, her maids were finished weaving the jewels through her hair and had attached the simple gold circlet of the heir. Samantha tried to take a deep breath, but was prevented by the tightness of her corset. "That's it. This is the last time I wear a corset. Have my dresses altered to fit without one. And don't lecture me about fashion. I'd rather be able to breathe."

Before her maids could protest that her breasts were small enough with a corset, she left the room. She passed through her reception room, which was decorated in a similar style to her bedroom and contained more ambassadorial gifts. She paused in front of her favorite tapestry—a white mare at the edge of the forest, helping her newborn foal stand. Wishing she was heading for the stables instead of the ballroom, she forced her face into a court smile and left her chambers.

Her two bodyguards bowed and fell in behind her. The princess couldn't remember a time when she hadn't been followed by two heavily armed men. She'd grown so used to them she often forgot they were there.

* * *

A full crowd tonight, of course. While the possibility of wearing a crown still exists, not even a deadly plague would keep the hordes away.

The princess entered the vast ballroom. Behind the dais at the top of the ballroom was the king's standard—a brilliant yellow sun on a field of red. Next to it was a smaller standard in her own colors — the head of a white horse on a field of emerald green. The walls were lined with the standards of all the noble houses of Korthlundia; most sported images of ferocious beasts or weapons of war. *If I'm supposed to be maintaining the peace, why do I have to dance in a room that celebrates war?* Her father claimed they couldn't redecorate the ballroom without the risk of offending one or more of the Korthlundian noble houses. But Samantha doubted she'd like balls any better no matter how the room was decorated.

As Samantha moved through the crowd, the courtiers parted and bowed. All the men attempted to catch her eye, and the smiles of the women failed to mask their jealousy.

She mounted the dais where her father and members of the royal council awaited. King Solar beamed at her. His long white hair and beard flowed around his head, giving him the appearance of the wise old man from the bards' tales. She bowed to him, and he quickly extended his hand, raised her, and gave her a kiss on the cheek. Despite his insistence that she marry, her father did love her. The princess knew she should consider herself lucky. Most royal children had no choice in a spouse, but her father had left her free to choose among the men of appropriate rank. But as she looked over the sea of hungry male eyes, the thought of marrying any of them nauseated her. *If only marrying them didn't mean I had to bed them.*

Beside the king, Uncle Caedmon smiled at her. Caedmon, Duke of Tuath and Boirche, was her mother's uncle and had been her father's chancellor since she was two years old. He had very bushy eyebrows that gave the impression he was always looking down on people. But he was one of the few members of her father's council she liked, and he was the only one who exhibited no designs on the throne. His only son had married before she was born.

Immediately after the king announced the opening of the ball, Argblutal, the Duke of Handgriff, stepped forward to claim the first dance. No one else ever dared ask her until the duke had had his turn. Like every Korthlundian man, Argblutal was tall, broad-shouldered, and blue-eyed. Many of the girls found him handsome. Samantha wasn't sure why. He was nearly twice her age. He was dressed in a surcoat of black leather with long black velvet sleeves, trimmed in gold and crimson braid. He had several thick gold chains around his neck. From the largest of these hung a pendant of a panther, the symbol of his house. In defiance of court fashion, he wore his blond beard and hair cropped short. He and Duke Sheen were her closest living relatives on her father's side, not that they were very close—third cousins or something. Both had thought to inherit the throne until her birth gave Solar a direct heir.

Argblutal bowed. "May I have the first dance, Your Highness?"

"I'd be honored, Your Grace." She smiled her fakest smile and accepted his hand.

As the dance began, the duke bowed low over her hand, sliming it with a kiss. "Your Highness, you are the brightest star in a shining crowd tonight." *It's only the first dance, and I get the star thing already. Is there some book they all read? Fifty-two Compliments for Ladies. A Beginner's Guide to Flattery.* The duke danced stiffly, as if he disapproved of frivolity. "Your dress, it's Saloynan silk, is it not, Your Highness?"

"No, it's Neasarian. I find the weave so much finer. Don't you?" The silk did feel delightful against her skin, but she found talk of fashion and fabric tedious. She'd never understood the other girls' obsession with it, just as she never understood why they giggled so much.

"So I have heard, Your Highness, but it's very difficult to come by. The Neasarians are more interested in trading spices than silk."

This was true, but equally boring, so she smiled and made some inane comment. When the dance finally ended,

Argblutal slimed her hand again. "Perhaps we can share another dance before the evening's end, Your Highness." Samantha merely smiled, surreptitiously wiping her hand on her gown. *Only if all seven of the hells freeze over.*

The next suitor in line was Lord Devyn, Duke Sheen's oldest son. Devyn was only a couple of years older than the princess, but he looked younger. His chin was covered with only the lightest and most delicate of fuzz. The princess thought he'd look better if he shaved. But, of course, he couldn't do that; only the clergy shaved. "May I . . . may I have this dance, Y-y-your Highness?"

As the dance began, Lord Devyn turned a dozen shades of red. "Y-y-your Highness looks just like a-a-a flower tonight." It was obvious he didn't want to dance any more than she did, but Duke Sheen was bent on controlling Korthlundia through his son. She'd heard the duke had threatened Devyn with the lash to force him to court her. Devyn was only comfortable among his paints and canvases. Besides, he was in love with Count Morfran's daughter, Lady Aislinn. She wished just once some man would look at her the way she'd seen Devyn look at Aislinn.

Samantha noticed blue under his fingernails. "And how is your latest creation coming. Working in blues, I see."

Devyn gaped. "I'm doing a seascape, Your Highness, but how could you know?" When she glanced at his fingers, he curled his fingernails into his fists. "Your Highness, how could I have been so neglectful? My father will kill me." Devyn was a nice boy, but she wished his father would leave him to his art and his lover.

After Devyn, the princess worked her way through her father's council—Count Kayne, Count Weylin, Baron Arawn's son, and a host of other nobles of varying degrees of importance. Nola, Count of Meillid, looked on wistfully. The count was nearly as round as he was tall, and it was rumored he'd do away with his wife if he thought he stood a chance of capturing the princess's hand. He had a five-year-old son, and Samantha thought it a wonder Nola didn't send the toddler to court her.

* * *

The king went to bed at midnight, but Samantha was forced to stay and dance with suitor after suitor.

"Might I dance with the stars of heaven tonight?" Count Pandaran, the only member of her father's council with whom she hadn't yet danced, asked. He always danced with her late in the balls; maybe he felt he was saving the best for last. He wore a surcoat of bright turquoise, edged with yards and yards of delicate lace. His hair and beard hung in long, blond ringlets. The princess smiled a court smile and took his hand. She cringed at the smoothness of his palms. *The damned fool doesn't even know how to wield a sword.* The hands of most of the men at court were like hers—rough and calloused from weapons training.

As they whirled around the ballroom floor, a soft glow of rotten orange erupted around Pandaran. A steaming heat seeped from the orange and poured over her, coating her body with a slime so thick a dozen baths wouldn't cleanse her. The princess nearly cried out in despair. *Not the colors again! I thought I'd gotten rid of them!* It had been several months since she'd spent all night kneeling at the altar in the palace chapel and praying for the goddess's help. She'd felt the goddess's peace and thought the terrifying colors gone forever. But again she'd been wrong. When she'd first seen the colors, she'd gone in disguise to the Temple of the Mother's Love. It was the only time she'd ever given her bodyguards the slip. She'd confessed her sins to a priest and told him about the colors. The priest had insisted she was under the influences of the denizens of darkness and that her soul was in great peril. He'd performed an exorcism, but it hadn't worked. Nothing had. *Maybe it's not demons; maybe I'm insane.*

The princess was so upset after her dance that she fled the room without giving an explanation. She ignored the questions from her bodyguards and her maids, but she was shaking by the time Ardra and Malvina had finished undressing her and taking down her hair. When she was finally alone, she curled up into a ball on her bed and prayed to the goddess.

ABOUT THE AUTHOR

From early childhood, Jamie has been immersed in books. Her mother, an avid reader, read to her, and her older sister filled her head with fairy tales. Taking into consideration her love for literature and the challenges of supporting herself as a writer, she pursued a Ph.D. in American literature, which she received in 1998. She started teaching writing and literature at Auburn University. But in doing so, she put her true passion on the backburner and neglected her muse. Then one day, in the midst of writing a piece of literary criticism, she realized that what she wanted to be doing was writing fantasy novels. Her muse thus revived, she began the book that was to become *The Goddess's Choice,* which was published in April 2012. Her third novel is soon to be released.

She lives in Auburn, Alabama, with her husband and four cats, which (or so she's been told) officially makes her a cat lady. She still teaches writing and literature at Auburn University. She is the mother of one grown son.

OTHER BOOKS BY JAMIE MARCHANT

The Kronicles of Korthlundia

> The Ghost in Exile (To be released soon)
> The Soul Stone (2015)
> The Goddess's Choice (2012)

Demons in the Big Easy: A Novella (2013)

Story Collections including her work

> *Of Dragons & Magic: Tales of Lost Worlds* (2014)
> *Urban Fantasy* (2013)
> *Best Genre Short Stories Anthology #2: Short Story.Me!*
> *(Volume 2)* (2010)

All works are available on Amazon.com and other online retailers. Autographed copies can be purchased directly from the author at www.jamie-marchant.com.

www.ingramcontent.com/pod-product-compliance
Lightning Source LLC
Chambersburg PA
CBHW070536130626
46555CB00003B/1447